Dr. King's Refrigerator

And Other Bedtime Stories

CHARLES JOHNSON

Scribner

NEW YORK   LONDON   TORONTO   SYDNEY

SCRIBNER
1230 Avenue of the Americas
New York, NY 10020

This book is a work of fiction. Names, characters, places, and
incidents either are products of the author's imagination or
are used fictitiously. Any resemblance to actual events or
locales or persons, living or dead, is entirely coincidental.

SCRIBNER and design are trademarks of
Macmillan Library Reference USA, Inc., used under license
by Simon & Schuster, the publisher of this work.

For information about special discounts for bulk purchases,
please contact Simon & Schuster Special Sales:
1-800-456-6798 or business@simonandschuster.com

DESIGNED BY KYOKO WATANABE
Text set in Fairfield

Manufactured in the United States of America

1   3   5   7   9   10   8   6   4   2

Library of Congress Cataloging-in-Publication Data

Johnson, Charles Richard, 1948–
Dr. King's refrigerator and other bedtime stories / Charles Johnson.
p. cm.
Contents: Sweet dreams—Cultural relativity—Dr. King's refrigerator—
The gift of the Osuo—Executive decision—Better than counting
sheep—The queen and the philosopher—Kwoon.
I. Title.
PS3560.O3735D69 2005
813'.54—dc22
2004056642

ISBN 0-7432-6453-3

ALSO BY CHARLES JOHNSON

FICTION

Soulcatcher and Other Stories

Dreamer

Middle Passage

The Sorcerer's Apprentice

Oxherding Tale

Faith and the Good Thing

PHILOSOPHY

Being and Race: Black Writing Since 1970

NONFICTION

King: The Photobiography of Martin Luther King Jr.
(with Bob Adelman)

I Call Myself an Artist:
Writings by and about Charles Johnson
(edited by Rudolph Byrd)

Africans in America
(with Patricia Smith)

Black Men Speaking
(with John McCluskey Jr.)

Turning the Wheel: Essays on Buddhism and Writing

Passing the Three Gates: Interviews with Charles Johnson
(edited by James McWilliams)

DRAWINGS

Half-Past Nation Time

Black Humor

*For the founders of the Charles Johnson Society
at the American Literature Association*

Contents

"The job of the artist is always to deepen the mystery."

—*Francis Bacon*

"Art flourishes where there is a sense of adventure."

—*Alfred North Whitehead*

"Reality can be beaten with enough imagination."

—*Mark Twain*

Dr. King's Refrigerator

Sweet Dreams

"PLEASE, COME IN. Sit down," he says. "I'm sorry I had to keep you waiting."

You cautiously enter the Auditor's tiny office, holding in your right hand the certified letter you received yesterday, the one that says "Department of Dream Revenue" in the upper-left-hand corner and, below that, the alarming words "Official Business." The letter had knocked you to your knees. It has been burning in your hand and giving you a headache and upsetting your stomach all day long. So it's almost a relief to finally be here, on the twentieth floor of a gray government building on First Avenue—almost as if you have been a fugitive from the law, running and hiding, and looking nervously over your shoulder. In fact, the letter said you *would* face prosecution if you didn't travel to downtown Seattle and take care of this business immediately. But now the anxiety is over.

You are there to pay your dream tax.

As administrative offices go, this one is hardly more than a cubicle. The furniture is identical to every other bureaucratic compartment in the building so that no government worker feels that he or she has been issued more or less than his or her coworkers. There is a cluttered desk, a wastebasket on top of which sits a cross-cut paper shredder, a small table containing a Muratec fax machine and a Xerox copier. At the rear of the room, a four-drawer filing cabinet is pushed against the wall. Resting on this is a small Dream Meter just like the one the government attached to your bed and *every*one's bed many years ago—a little black box roughly the size of a cell phone, with an LCD that digitally reads out the number of dreams you have on any given night, their duration, category, and the fee assigned for each one. Not being a very technical person, you're not sure exactly how the Dream Meter works, but you *do* know there is a hefty fine for tampering with it—greater than for tampering with a smoke detector in an airplane's toilet—

and somehow the Dream Meter works in conjunction with the microscopic implant your doctor inserted in your neck through a hypodermic needle, using the same process by which stray dogs are given their own bar code for identification at the city's animal shelter. To the left of the cabinet, on which sits the Dream Meter, is a calendar turned to today's October twenty-first-century date.

"Can I get you anything?" the Auditor asks. "Coffee? Tea?" When you tell him that no, you're fine, he sits back in his chair, which creaks a little. He is a pale young man; his color is that of plaster, perhaps because he sits all day in this windowless cubicle. You place his age at thirty. Thirty-five. He has blond hair, perfect teeth, and wears a pinstriped shirt with the sleeves rolled up to his elbows. All in all, he seems anonymous, like the five hundred other bureaucrats in cubicles just like this one—like functionaries in Terry Gilliam's movie *Brazil*—but your Auditor has tried his best to personalize and give a bit of panache to both his office and himself. He wears a brightly colored Jerry Garcia tie. On his desk where your dream file wings open, he has a banker's lamp with a green glass shade on a solid brass base. And he wears a ring watch on his right index finger. A bit of ostentatious style, you think. Something that speaks to his having a smidgen of imagination, maybe even an adventurous, eccentric spirit beneath the way the State has swallowed his individuality. Right then you decide your Auditor is someone like you, a person who is just trying to do his job and, who knows, maybe he really understands your problem and wants to help you.

"Is this your first audit?" he asks.

You tell him that yes, it is.

"Well, don't worry," he says. "I'll try to make this as painless as possible for you. Have you been read your rights as a taxpayer?"

You nod your head, yes. His assistant in the outer office did that.

"And," he asks, "did she inform you that if you fail to make a full payment today—or make arrangements to pay in installments—that we can take your pay-check, your bank account, your car, or your house? Did she explain that?"

For a moment your heart tightens in your chest. You feel the sudden desire to stand and run scream-ing out of this airless room, but instead you bite down on your lower lip and bob your head up and down.

The Auditor says, "Good. Don't be nervous. You're doing fine. And I assure you, everything we say here is confidential." He peers down at the paperwork on his desk. Slowly, his smile begins to fade. "Our records show a discrepancy in the amount of dream tax that you paid last year. You declared on form ten-sixty that you enjoyed the experience of three hundred and sixty-five dreams during the previous tax period. But your Dream Meter recorded five hundred and seventy-five dreams during that time. Dreams, I regret to say, for which you did not pay. Do you have an explanation?"

Now the room has begun to blur and shimmer like something seen through a haze of heat. You feel perspiration starting at your temples, and you tug on your shirt collar, knowing the Auditor is right. You tell him you *love* to dream. One of your greatest pleasures is the faint afterglow of a good dream once it's over, the lingering, mysterious images as wispy and ethereal as smoke, which you try to hang on to for the rest of the day, tasting them like the memory of a delicious meal, or a secret you can't share with anyone else. You tell him you enjoy taking a nap in the late afternoon, a siesta like they do in Spain, and that's why your Dream Meter reading is so high. You thought only dreams at bedtime counted. You didn't know naps in the daytime counted too.

"They do—and so do daydreams," he says. "You neglected to declare one hundred and eighty dreams experienced during naps. This is a *serious* offense. Ignorance is no excuse for breaking the law. By my computation, you owe the Department of Dream

Revenue ninety-one thousand, six hundred and forty-five dollars and fourteen cents."

That much? you say.

"Yes, I'm afraid so," he says. "The amount of your dreams places you in a thirty-three percent tax bracket." From his desk he lifts a sheet of paper that details your dream underpayments and a long column of dates. "Do you see this?" he says. "Your actual underpayment comes to fifty thousand dollars. But we charged you a penalty because, according to our records, you did not estimate the dreams you intended to have and pay the correct amount of tax due. You did not file for an extension. Furthermore, that payment is now two years late. So we had to charge you interest. I must say that a few of your dreams were very lavish and long running. They were in Technicolor. Some of them were better than the movies at Blockbuster. You *do* have a vivid imagination. And you should be thankful for that. Did you know that in a few Native American cultures, dreams are seen as an extension of waking consciousness, that a dreamer considers his visions when he's sleeping to be as much a part of his history as the things he experiences when he's awake?"

No, you say. You weren't aware of that.

"You know," he says, "I especially enjoyed that dream of yours where you find yourself shipwrecked on an island in the South Pacific, with no one there but you and a whole tribe of beautiful women who play a game of tossing a golden ball back and forth to each other. I've been thinking about that. Do you suppose the ship that goes down, the one you escaped from, symbolizes your job? But I can't figure out—in terms of Freud, Reich, or Maslow—what that damned golden ball means."

You tell him you don't know what it means either. But the night you had that dream, just before you went to bed, you were reading Homer's *Odyssey,* the part where Odysseus meets Nausicaä and sojourns among the Phaeacians.

"Oh, *that* explains it then." With his fingers the Auditor makes a steeple as he leans forward, nodding. "That one dream cost you five hundred dollars. You should be more careful about what you read at bedtime. Well, let's get back to business. We have all your dreams recorded. I've reviewed each one, of course. Recurrent dreams—like the one where you marry your high school's homecoming queen—*those* must be taxed at twice the rate of regular dreams. Nightmares, like the one where your mother-in-law comes to live with you and your wife forever, or the one where you are giving a presentation to your company's board of directors and discover you are naked, are taxed three times higher. And it shows here that you had sixty-seven undeclared wet dreams, which—as you know—place you in a higher tax bracket. Does all this make sense to you? Do you wish to contest anything I've said?"

No, you say, you won't argue. You *did* do all that dreaming. But you tell him you can't afford to pay that amount. That it will devastate your savings, maybe drive you into the poorhouse. You will have to borrow money from friends. Take out a second mortgage on your home . . .

The eyes of your Auditor soften for a second when he hears that. He sits back in his chair again, folding his hands, and sighs. "I know, I know. Those who dream more always pay more. I wish to God I could help. All I can do, in my official capacity, is explain the situation to you."

Please, you say. How did all this come about?

He says, "Oh, that's easy to answer. The Dream Tax started early in this century. In Seattle voters were presented with a ballot measure that would cut vehicle license fees to thirty dollars and require public votes on all state and local tax and fee increases. The initiative failed, but passed a decade later in its entirety. And not just in Seattle. It passed all over the country and exacerbated a revenue crisis that had been worsening every year since September eleven, two thousand one, what with the collapse of the high-tech industry, a deepening recession, the bailout of the airlines, the rebuilding of New York, and an open-ended global campaign against terrorism. A new source of revenue was needed to fund all kinds of domestic projects, homeland security, and public works—highway maintenance, public health programs, day care centers, and so forth.

"We had to start thinking outside the box, as they used to say. To find a way to tax intangibles like thought itself. There, you see, was a vast, unexploited realm for underwriting public works and salvaging the national treasury—dreams, subjective phenomenon, and the immaterial products of the soul. The bureaucrat who dreamed it up remains nameless to this day, and he was, of course, taxed for his stroke of brilliance. But that was the beginning. As the old saying goes, necessity is the mother of invention. Once the need was clear, the Dream Tax, and all the technology to support it, were rushed into place in a matter of months."

The Auditor pauses to reach into his desk drawer and remove a receipt book. "Now, will you be paying by check or in cash?"

A check, you say, wearily. In fact, you already have it written out, and hand it over to the Auditor, asking him if he can perhaps work with you a little on the payment by waiting a day or two before the Department of Dream Revenue cashes it.

"Yes," he says, smiling. "That's the least we can do. After all, we are here to be helpful."

Just then the room seems to tilt, leaning to the left like a ship on tempestuous waves. You squeeze the bridge of your nose with two fingers to steady yourself until this spell of dizziness passes. Then you turn to leave, but stop suddenly in the doorway because there is one final question you need to ask.

Does he, the Auditor, *dream?*

"Me?" he says, touching his chest with two fingers. "Dream? Oh, no, I can't afford it." He looks at your check, smiles again, and slips it into the top drawer in his desk. "Everything seems to be in order, at least for now. You have a good day, sir. Thank you. And sweet dreams . . ."

Cultural Relativity

Not long ago a college student named Felicia Brooks felt she was the most fortunate young woman in all Seattle, and possibly in the entire world, except for one small problem.

She was deeply in love with her boyfriend, an African student who was the only son of his country's president. His name was Fortunata Maafa. In the spring of 2001, they both were graduating seniors at the University of Washington. They had been dating all year long, he was *more* than she could ever have hoped for, and Felicia knew all her friends thought Fortunata was catnip. In fact, she was afraid sometimes that they might steal him from her. Most of them had given up on black men entirely. Or at least they had given up on American black men. Their mantra, which Felicia had heard a thousand times, and often chanted herself, was, "All the *good* black men are taken, and the rest are in prison, on drugs, or unemployed, or dating white women—or don't like girls at all." What was a sistah to do? During high school and college, Felicia and her friends despaired of ever finding Mr. Right.

But then, miraculously, she met Fortunata fall quarter at the Langston Hughes Cultural Center. He looked like a young Kwame Nkrumah, he dressed as elegantly as Michael Jordan, was gorgeous the few times she saw him in his *agbada* (African robe), and he fit George Bernard Shaw's definition of a gentleman being "a man who always tries to put in a little more than he takes out." Furthermore, he was rich. He could play the *kora*, an African stringed instrument, so beautifully you'd cry. Yet, for all that, he still had a schoolboy shyness and was frequently confused by the way Americans did things, especially by pop culture, which was so sexually frank compared to his own country that it made Fortunata squirm. All of this Felicia thought was charming as well as exciting because it meant he was her very own Galatea, and she was his Pygmalion, his guide and interpreter on these shores. He dazzled her every day when he described the ancient culture of his father's kingdom in West Africa. There, in that remote world, his people were introducing the most sophisticated technology, and that was why Fortunata had studied computer engineering. But, he said, his people worked hard to avoid the damaging aspects of Westernization. They were determined to revolutionize their science, but also to preserve their thousand-year-old traditions, their religion, and their folkways, even when the reason for some of these unique practices had been forgotten.

One night in June after their final exams were over, Felicia played for him the movie *Coming to America* on the VCR in her studio apartment on Capital Hill, hoping he would enjoy it, which he did. No sooner was it over, than Fortunata slid closer to her on the sofa, and said, "I am *so* like Eddie Murphy in this funny movie. I came to America four years ago, not just for an education, but really to find a beautiful American woman to share my life. To be my queen. Felicia, that woman is *you*, if you will have me. Because if I can't have you, then I don't want anyone. I just won't marry, ever."

Naturally, Felicia said yes.

"And," he added, "you promise not to change your mind? No matter what happens?"

She did.

From the pocket of his suitcoat, Fortunata produced a ring with a flawless, four-carat diamond shaped like the Star of South Africa, for precious stones were plentiful in his country, a nation rich in natural resources. Felicia threw her arms around him. Then, without thinking, acting on what she believed was instinct, she brought her lips close to his. But before she could kiss Fortunata, he wiggled away.

"*What?*" said Felicia. "What's wrong?"

Fortunata gave her a shy, sideways look. His voice trembled. "I'm *so* sorry. We don't do that. . . ."

What?" she said. "You don't kiss?"

She looked straight at him, he looked down. "You know I can't."

"*Why* not?"

"Please, don't start this again." Now Fortunata seemed nervous; he began rolling the end of his tie between his fingers. "I'm not *sure* why. We just don't. The reason is lost in antiquity. Felicia, it's not that unusual. Polynesians rub noses, you know. Samoans sniff each other. And traditional Japanese and Chinese cultures did not include this strange practice called *kissing*. I suspect they felt it was *too* intimate a thing for people to do. All I know is that my father warned me never to do this thing when I came to America. We've discussed this before. Don't you remember?"

Felicia did remember, but not happily. This was the *one* thing about Fortunata that baffled and bothered her deeply. She understood that his culture was very traditional. For example, Fortunata's people insisted that sex should be postponed until a couple's wedding night. All during the past year, they'd done almost *every*thing else that lovers did. They held hands, hugged, and snuggled. But there were *no* kisses. Not even an air kiss. Or a good-night kiss when he dropped Felicia off at her apartment and returned to his dormitory. The last thing she wanted was to be culturally insensitive, or to offend Fortunata, or to have him break off their nearly perfect relationship. So on those past occasions, Felicia never insisted that he kiss her. Nor did she insist on the night he summoned up the courage to propose.

After taking a deep breath, she said, sadly, "Can we rub noses then?"

"Of course," said Fortunata. "I think *that's* okay."

It is well known that when two people fall in love, their brains produce an amphetaminelike substance (phenylethylamines) that is responsible for what we call "lover's high." After Fortunata left, Felicia still felt this chemically created elixir of strong emotion; but she also felt very confused. What she felt, in fact, was half ecstasy that she was to wed the son of an African statesman, and half bewilderment because rubbing noses—in her view—was no substitute for a big wet one. She was a highly intelligent woman. A woman about to graduate with a degree in anthropology. She wondered if she was being culturally inflexible. But Felicia knew that all her life she had been fascinated by and respectful of the differences in cultures, how each was a self-contained and complete system that must be understood from within. She knew her Levi-Strauss and the work of dozens of structural anthropologists. You did not have to tell her that in some Muslim countries, it was insulting to cross your legs when sitting if the soles of your shoes were displayed to your host. Or that in Theravada Buddhist countries like Thailand, patting a cute youngster on the top of his head was a no-no because that part of the body was looked upon as sacred. So yes, she had always taken great pains to listen carefully when Fortunata spoke of his country's history and mysterious customs.

But she *wanted* a kiss! Was that asking for so much?

In her heart she *knew* that kissing was special, and to prove it to herself, she sat down at her computer, went to the Internet, and spent the night looking at everything she could find on the subject. Just as she'd expected, kissing as an expression of love and affection was old. Very old. It dated back to the fifth century. And as a custom, it was even older than that! The early Christians borrowed kissing from the Romans. Clearly, it was the most *human* of practices. Everyone knew animals didn't kiss. They licked. The reason for *having* lips in the first place, Felicia decided just before daybreak, was so people could use their God-given soup coolers as the most romantic, the most erotic, and the most natural way to show they loved someone.

During the last year Felicia had introduced Fortunata to all kinds of things outside his culture—karaoke, the music of Jimi Hendrix and Kurt Cobain, the importance of Ichiro bobbleheads, and why everyone needed a good-looking tattoo—and he had enjoyed *all* of it, and thanked her for enlightening him, as a good Galatea would. When she finally drifted off to sleep, around ten A.M., Felicia wondered if Fortunata had lied. That maybe people in his culture *did* kiss, but for some reason he simply didn't want to kiss *her*. But, no! She had never caught him in a lie before. It was more likely that he'd never kissed *any*one. So she was certain that if Fortunata could just experience the electric thrill of kissing *once*, and with the right woman (meaning herself), then a wonderful new cultural doorway would open for him. If she truly loved him, Felicia knew she owed him that.

As luck would have it, Fortunata dropped by unexpectedly that evening as she was fixing dinner. He was almost bursting with excitement.

"Felicia," he said, "I just spoke with my father. I told him about our engagement. We have his blessing. In my country the wedding ceremony lasts for a week. Since my father is president, the whole country will celebrate." He paused to catch his breath. "Aren't you happy?"

To show her happiness, Felicia pressed her body against him. Before he could move, she placed her hands on both sides of his head, pulled him closer, puckered up, and bestowed upon a startled Fortunata the most soulful, moist, and meaningful lip lock she had ever delivered in her life. She felt her heart beating faster, the temperature of her skin beneath her clothes heating up. Smiling, Felicia took a step back. The expression on Fortunata's face was unreadable. He started to speak, but stopped.

And then, suddenly, he was gone.

Where Fortunata had stood there was a full-grown, giant West African frog. It was a foot long and weighed as much as a fox terrier.

"I warned you," he said.

Felicia felt ill. She thought, *I can't handle this.* But what she said was:

"I don't suppose we can break off the engagement, can we?"

"Don't be silly," said the frog.

Dr. King's Refrigerator

अन्नद् भवन्ति भुतानि
Beings exist from food.

—*Bhagavad-Gita*, Book 3, Chapter 14

IN SEPTEMBER, the year of Our Lord 1954, a gifted young minister from Atlanta named Martin Luther King Jr. accepted his first pastorate at the Dexter Avenue Baptist Church in Montgomery, Alabama. He was twenty-five years old, and in the language of the Academy, he took his first job when he was ABD at Boston University's School of Theology—All *But* *Dissertation*—which is a common and necessary practice for scholars who have completed their course work and have families to feed. If you are offered a job when still in graduate school, you snatch it, and, if all goes well, you finish the thesis that first year of your employment when you are in the thick of things, trying mightily to prove—in Martin's case— to the staid, high-toned laity at Dexter that you really are worth the $4,800 salary they were paying you. He had, by the way, the highest-paying job of any minister in the city of Montgomery, and the expectations for his daily performance—as pastor, husband, community leader, and son of Daddy King—were equally high.

But what few people tell the eager ABD is how completing the doctorate from a distance means wall-to-wall work. There were always meetings with the local NAACP, ministers' organizations, and church committees; or, failing that, the budget and treasury to balance; or, failing that, the sick to visit in their homes, the ordination of deacons to preside over, and a new sermon to write *every* week. During that first year away from Boston, he delivered forty-six sermons to his congregation, and twenty sermons and lectures at other colleges and churches in the South. And, dutifully, he got up every morning at five-thirty to spend three hours composing the dissertation in his parsonage, a white frame house with a railed-in front porch and two oak trees in the yard, after which he devoted another three hours to it late at night, in addition to spending sixteen hours each week on his Sunday sermons.

On the Wednesday night of December first, exactly one year before Rosa Parks refused to give up her bus seat, and after a long day of meetings and writing memos and letters, he sat entrenched behind a roll-top desk in his cluttered den at five minutes past midnight, smoking cigarettes and drinking black coffee, wearing an old fisherman's knit sweater, his desk barricaded in by books and piles of paperwork. Naturally, his in-progress dissertation, "A Comparison of the Conceptions of God in the Thinking of Paul Tillich and Henry Nelson Wieman," was itching at the edge of his mind, but what he really needed this night was a theme for his sermon on Sunday. Usually, by Tuesday Martin had at least a sketch, by Wednesday he had his research and citations— which ranged freely over five thousand years of Eastern and Western philosophy—compiled on note cards, and by Friday he was writing his text on a pad of lined yellow paper. Put bluntly, he was two days behind schedule.

A few rooms away, his wife was sleeping under a blue corduroy bedspread. For an instant he thought of giving up work for the night and climbing into sheets warmed by her body, curling up beside this beautiful and very understanding woman, a graduate of the New England Conservatory of Music, who had sacrificed her career back East in order to follow him into the Deep South. He remembered their wedding night on June eighteenth a year ago in Perry County, Alabama, and how the insanity of segregation meant he and his new bride could not stay in a hotel operated by whites. Instead, they spent their wedding night at a black funeral home and had no honeymoon at all. Yes, he probably *should* join her in their bedroom. He wondered if she resented how his academic and theological duties took him away from her and their home (many an ABD's marriage ended before the dissertation was done)—work like that infernal unwritten sermon, which hung over his head like the sword of Damocles.

Weary, feeling guilty, he pushed back from his desk, stretched out his stiff spine, and decided to get a midnight snack.

Now, he *knew* he shouldn't do that, of course. He often told friends that food was his greatest weakness. His ideal weight in college was 150 pounds, and he was aware that, at 5 feet, 7 inches tall, he should not eat between meals. His bantam weight ballooned easily. Moreover, he'd read somewhere that the average American will in his (or her) lifetime eat sixty thousand pounds of food. To Martin's ethical way of thinking, consuming that much tonnage was downright obscene, given the fact that there was so much famine and poverty throughout the rest of the world. He made himself a promise—a small prayer—to eat just a little, only enough tonight to replenish his tissues.

He made his way cautiously through the dark, seven-room house, his footsteps echoing on the hardwood floors as if he was in a swimming pool, scuffing from the smoke-filled den to the living room, where he circled around the baby-grand piano his wife practiced on for church recitals, then past her choices in decoration—two African masks on one wall and West Indian gourds on the mantel above the fireplace—to the kitchen. There, he clicked on the overhead light, then drew open the door to their refrigerator.

Scratching his stomach, he gazed—and gazed—at four well-stocked shelves of food. He saw a Florida grapefruit and a California orange. On one of the middle shelves he saw corn and squash, both native to North America, and introduced by Indians to Europe in the fifteenth century through Columbus. To the right of that, his eyes tracked bright yellow slices of pineapple from Hawaii, truffles from England, and a half-eaten Mexican tortilla. Martin took a step back, cocking his head to one side, less hungry now than curious about what his wife had found at a public market, and stacked inside their refrigerator without telling him.

He began to empty the refrigerator and heavily packed food cabinets, placing everything on the table and kitchen counter and, when those were filled, on the flower-printed linoleum floor, taking things out slowly at first, his eyes squinted, scrutinizing each item like an old woman on a fixed budget at the bargain table in a grocery store. Then he worked quickly, bewitched, chuckling to himself as he tore apart his wife's tidy, well-scrubbed, Christian kitchen. He removed all the berylline olives from a thick glass jar and held each one up to the light, as if perhaps he'd never really *seen* an olive before, or seen one so clearly. Of one thing he was sure: No two olives were the same. Within fifteen minutes Martin stood surrounded by a galaxy of food.

From one corner of the kitchen floor to the other, there were popular American items such as pumpkin pie and hot dogs, but also heavy, sour-sweet dishes like German sauerkraut and schnitzel right beside Tibetan rice, one of the staples of the Far East, all sorts of spices, and the macaroni, spaghetti, and ravioli favored by Italians. There were bricks of cheese and wine from French vineyards, coffee from Brazil, and from China and India black and green teas that probably had been carried from fields to faraway markets on the heads of women, or the backs of donkeys, horses, and mules. All of human culture, history, and civilization laid unscrolled at his feet, and he had only to step into his kitchen to discover it. No one people or tribe, living in one place on this planet, could produce the endless riches for the palate that he'd just pulled from his refrigerator. He looked around the disheveled room, and he saw in each succulent fruit, each slice of bread, and each grain of rice a fragile, inescapable network of mutuality in which all earthly creatures were codependent, integrated, and tied in a single garment of destiny. He recalled Exodus 25:30, and realized that all this before him was showbread. From the floor Martin picked up a Golden Delicious apple, took a bite from it, and instantly prehended the heat from summers past, the roots of the tree from which the fruit had been taken, the cycles of sun and rain and seasons, the earth, and even those who tended the orchard. Then he slowly put the apple down, feeling not so much hunger now as a profound indebtedness and thanksgiving—to everyone and everything in Creation. For was not *he* too the product of infinite causes and the full, miraculous orchestration of Being stretching back to the beginning of time?

At that moment his wife came into the disaster area that was their kitchen, half asleep, wearing blue slippers and an old housecoat over her nightgown. When she saw what her philosopher husband had done, she said, *Oh!* And promptly disappeared from the room. A moment later she was back, having composed herself and put on her glasses, but her voice was barely above a whisper:

"Are you all right?"

"Of course, I am! I've *never* felt better!" he said. "The whole universe is inside our refrigerator!"

She blinked.

"Really? You don't mean that, do you? Honey, have you been drinking? I've told you time and again that that orange juice and vodka you like so much isn't good for you, and if anyone at church smells it on your breath—"

"If you *must* know, I was hard at work on my dissertation an hour ago. I didn't drink a drop of *any*-thing—except coffee."

"Well, that explains," she said.

"No, you don't understand! I was trying to write my speech for Sunday, but—but—I couldn't think of anything, and I got hungry . . ."

She stared at the food heaped on the floor. "*This* hungry?"

"Well, *no*." His mouth wobbled, and now he was no longer thinking about the metaphysics of food but, instead, of how the mess he'd made must look through her eyes. And, more important, how *he* must look through her eyes. "I think I've got my sermon, or at least something I might use later. It's so obvious to me now!" He could tell by the tilt of her head and the twitching of her nose that she didn't think any of this was obvious at all. "When we get up in the morning, we go into the bathroom where we reach for a sponge provided for us by a Pacific Islander. We reach for soap created by a Frenchman. The towel is provided by a Turk. Before we leave for our jobs, we are beholden to more than half the world."

"Yes, dear." She sighed. "I can *see* that, but what about my kitchen? You *know* I'm hosting the Ladies Prayer Circle today at eight o'clock. That's seven hours from now. Please tell me you're going to clean up everything before you go to bed."

"But I have a sermon to write! What I'm saying— *trying* to say—is that whatever affects *one* directly, affects *all* indirectly!"

"Oh, yes, I'm sure all this is going to have a remarkable effect on the Ladies Prayer Circle—"

"Sweetheart . . ." He held up a grapefruit and a head of lettuce, "I had a *revelation* tonight. Do you know how rare that is? Those things don't come easy. Just ask Meister Eckhart or Martin Luther—you know Luther experienced enlightenment on the toilet, don't you? Ministers only get maybe one or two revelations in a lifetime. But *you* made it possible for me to have a vision when I opened the refrigerator." All at once, he had a discomfiting thought. "How much *did* you spend for groceries last week?"

"I bought extra things for the Ladies Prayer Circle," she said. "Don't ask how much and I won't ask why you've turned the kitchen inside out." Gracefully, like an angel, or the perfect wife in the Book of Proverbs, she stepped toward him over cans and containers, plates of leftovers and bowls of chili. She placed her hand on his cheek, like a mother might do with her gifted and exasperating child, a prodigy who had just torched his bedroom in a scientific experiment. Then she wrapped her arms around him, slipped her hands under his sweater, and gave him a good, long kiss—by the time they were finished, her glasses were fogged. Stepping back, she touched the tip of his nose with her finger, and turned to leave. "Don't stay up too late," she said. "Put everything back before it spoils. And come to bed—I'll be waiting."

Martin watched her leave and said, "Yes, dear,"

still holding a very spiritually understood grapefruit in one hand and an ontologically clarified head of lettuce in the other. He started putting everything back on the shelves, deciding as he did so that while his sermon could wait until morning, his new wife definitely should not.

The Gift of the Osuo

THE ALLMUSERI, an ancient African people whose kingdom once lay between Cape Lopez and the mouth of the Congo River, required any villager who desired to lead them to feed them foofoo and malt beer every third market, a custom that, according to our elders who never say the thing that is Not, limited Allmuseri rulers to a few generous and gentle men like the good Muslim king Shabaka Malik al Muhammad (1632–1688). This, after a fashion, is a fairy tale of their history.

A kind, large-bellied king, Shabaka scheduled few,

if any, fireside chats with his people because he was shy, and spluttered and blew spittle when speaking, which embarrassed his wife (everything he did embarrassed Queen Melle, to hear him tell it). Having heard an argument as to whether, say, yohimbe roots aided the digestion better than yams, and having made up his mind for yams, Shabaka forgot the spiraling steps of the argument, remembering only that he had a vague feeling of dislike for yohimbe roots, though he couldn't precisely tell you why. In a word, he was a tired, middle-aged king who lived quietly, knowing he would never be a chief of any importance if he lived to the age of elephants. Still, he knew he had the good fortune to be a sensibly balanced man with simple feelings and, like any good African king, winged his prayers aloft to Allah for greater patience and wisdom.

One day King Shabaka heard the sound of Mahdi and Kangabar, two *osuo*—sorcerers—arguing hotly outside his hut, which sat amiddlemost a circle of rain-whitened mud houses on a hill overlooking a river. Him they asked to settle a head-breaking dispute.

Now King Shabaka's day had been sour. The queen had shrieked at him, saying he cared not a whit for her because her womb was dry as bone. To do him justice, Shabaka did love his queen (when he didn't think too much about it), although she was sharp tongued and often snapped at him, as if he were not a king but instead a commoner of no consequence at all. His mind wandered, now and then, to memories of a younger girl named Noi, a griot's daughter, very beautiful. And very dead. Before his marriage Shabaka ordered his advisors Nduku, Bompo, and Tempo (all incompetents, according to the king) to "Find me for my wife the loveliest woman in the village." They hunted, fell into a squabble because they had no common standard of beauty, and Noi was married to a blacksmith. He was coarse and crude; and besides being coarse and crude, he abused Noi until her *kra* went to that place no man has visited. In other words, King Shabaka married, like so many men, not the woman who most stormed his senses, but the simple woman who would have a man as plain as himself. So it was that, at age sixty, King Shabaka, short-winded and feeling cheated, lived alongside but not exactly with his queen, who—if the truth be told—often asked Allah to sneeze her into the afterworld where her faith and loving kindness would be better appreciated.

He granted his sorcerers' an audience. "But speak quickly," sighed the king. "I am old, have no children, and verily I am married to a crone. Men such as I have little time for trifles."

Mahdi, brittle and serious in his leather cap and robe, was as bald as a stone, having around his head a few puffballs of gray hair like pothers of smoke. He said, "King, it seems to me that in disputes about the superiority of Mind and Matter, we must choose Matter because, as any clearheaded man will tell you, Matter is the only reality—hugely here, recalcitrant, resisting our desires, indifferent to what we think about it; here even, O King, when we cease to think and change our houses." He looked up from beneath a brow that beetled out over his tiny eyes. "What say you, King? Do I speak well?"

Shabaka squeezed the bridge of his nose with two fingers, a sign that he was thinking. These arrogant wizards, these vain grammarians often seemed as mad to him as the full moon. They studied the bezoar stones in the numbles of oxen and preached cracked doctrines that, unchecked, might unleash mischief in the world. The king thought slowly, and said, "Mahdi, you are right."

"That's not it at *all*," said Kangabar, who was bearded and stared straight ahead at Shabaka, unblinking, like a fish. "Mind is primary, O King," he said, puffing breath scented with porridgy millet beer at Shabaka. "For what can we know that is not, first and foremost, filtered—do you follow me?—through the sieve of the Mind." So he spoke.

Shabaka listened, pulling at his fingers. His thoughts lazed in the room, alighting on a huge jug of zythum. "That too sounds pretty good."

"King," objected Mahdi, a little miffed. He was staring at the bulbous knot of Shabaka's navel. "You must choose *between* these antinomies!"

Kangabar added, "Yes, a world view is at stake. These things can't be—you're not listening again— taken lightly. If I am right, then all I see has a smattering of me in it. But if Mahdi is right"—he shot the other a slow, sideways look—"then all is lost, King— we sojourn in a soulless world of pure mechanics: *click, click, click!*"

"Horrible!" The king rubbed his chin. "Give me a second to think."

Because Shabaka was a good king, which merely means that he sought the glue that from olden times had held things together among the Allmuseri, he took both their hands and said, "You are both right. Without Matter, my dear friend Mahdi, surely there is no Mind; the *I* would be an empty mirror. But you, Kangabar, are also right, for without Mind, there is no sensible world. We see our human reflection, flawed as it is, echoed back in every spear of grass and baobob tree. We are informed and give form at the same time." King Shabaka found his speech, one of the longest he'd given, so sweet when he'd finished (he had, it's true, been groping for an answer, afraid he'd fail or waffle the issue, when—revelation!—the sounds strung themselves together nicely on their own natural rhythms, creating sense where he'd expected none) that he smiled and said, "So I conclude that thought and things originally are of the same species."

The sorcerers were delighted with this democratic solution. So delighted, in fact, that from the folds of his fusty robe Mahdi's fingers withdrew a length of charcoal as thick as three fingers. This he handed to the king. "To show our appreciation," he said, "we offer you this gift to please your nieces and nephews. This chalk is ten years older than Allah himself. Whatever you sketch with this shall leap hugely to life."

"Inshallah!" Shabaka took the chalk tentatively, as though it might sting him. "*Any*thing, I heard you say?"

Mahdi and Kangabar smiled exactly like twin chimpanzees. They bowed, promised to remember Shabaka in their prayers, and, arguing again, scuffed back outside. As for King Shabaka, he stared and stared at the strip of charcoal, sputtered, "Ridiculous! Am I a child to believe in enchanted chalk?" Then he chortled and made answer, "Perhaps . . ." With torturously slow motion, for King Shabaka was no artist, he squatted on his hams, stuck his tongue between his brown teeth, and traced on the southern wall of his hut an eleven-cubit-long, golden-shafted spear with a head of silver—a spear such as only lives in legends and old hero myths, and, lo, his crude ideogram thickened, filled out like a blowfish, and fell clattering from the wall to his dirt floor, leaving where it had been a slight burn that smelled of sulphur mingled with cork. "There is no Majesty and there is no Might," bellowed the king, trembling, "save in Allah, the Great, the Glorious!" He shut his eyes. He looked again. It was still there. King Shabaka weighed the spear in his hand, shouldered it, then squeezed the charcoal in his pudgy fist, laughing nervously now, for he was not perfectly sober at the sight of such wizardry. "Truly," he thought, "this is no toy for my nieces and nephews."

At once the unhappy king shut himself away in his hut, where no women and only a few advisors were admitted, and spent his whole day drawing the impala and zebra skins prized by his people; he sketched smooth-muscled horses with frothy sweat on their withers and finely dight in heavy saddles, blood dromedaries, and trumpeting she elephants, herds of blorting cattle, cows with full udders splashing milk to the ground, ya-honking birds, and other creatures of the animal and spirit worlds—elementals and ifrits—which, when he left his hut that evening, followed boldly out behind the king like beasts fleeing a flood. All these Shabaka gave to his people. But, mind you, there was no mimesis here: Shabaka's animals resembled not the Real, but the Real transfigured (which is the origin of all beauty, all art).

As the night drew on, King Shabaka doodled by the flimmer of a palm-oil lamp the elder gods and goddesses worshiped by his people before Islam swept across the African continent; he drew shades not seen on earth since the beginning of time. They talked with Shabaka, chided him for falling short of the greatness of his grandfathers, and, at last bored with the king's goggling at them, went visibly into the world. (Shabaka, to speak truly, was relieved to see them go.) He drew battalions of men with bark shields, which all came to life and saluted him. "Hail! Hail to the king!" Shabaka cackled like a child. He drew three musicians with neginoths and marimbas who played for him, but as they made music the melancholy strains suggested to the unhappy king— as well you might imagine—the dead girl Noi, whose memory grew like a knot at the front of Shabaka's brow, where the humors for imagination lie. Glum, chewing his gums, the king sniffled and, as his musicians played, sketched her likeness on his plastered wall.

Miraculously, Noi stepped naked as a Shami apple from the wall, emerging like a figure entering the world through a magic mirror.

"Oh, my goodness!" cried the king. He came to his feet clapping his hands and blowing spittle. Noi stood with her hands shielding her breasts. King Shabaka knuckled his eyes. "Surely," he said, "I am dead or dreaming!"

"I am Noi," said this vision. She bowed, then added, "To hear is to obey."

The musicians stopped playing. One of them said—a sigh—"Inshallah!"

"Get out! Get out!" Shabaka dismissed his musicians, blew out the light, and looked at the smooth molding of Noi's back and shoulders. She had been carried, long ago, sheathed in an animal skin on a wooden stretcher to a beehive behind the village, where the dead were eaten—King Shabaka remembered that clearly. Even so, she stood here now. And in all the world, there was not a more beautiful woman than Noi. She had eyes black as obsidian, and features like those of an Ur figure poised at the misty, mythical beginnings of the race before the earth and sea were separated. The king clamped shut his eyes. He would have given her a goodly stroke right then if, from outside, he had not heard the queen's rattling voice call his name.

"Shabaka? Sha-ba-kaaa!" (Her voice made the air around his head jump.) "Shabaka Malik al Muhammad, is that you in there?" (The king sat hunched in the corner as though waiting for a tree to fall.) "Shabaka, who's talking to you?"

Now it ill-befits a king to curse, but Shabaka did so. Then he scrawled an ugly cartoon of the queen, all nose and kneecaps, and after that one of Noi's husband, then he x-ed them out, which snapped off Queen Melle's shrill warbling as though she'd been strangled. He dusted off his hands. His head was light. Placing the chalk aside, he took Noi by the hand, drew her to him, gave her as good a stroke as possible for a man of advanced middle age, then, dismounting from her bosom, slept and snored and snarked. Noi's head pillowed on his arm as he lay tangled in nightmares that he had killed the queen, the village blacksmith, conjured up the dead, and slept with a corpse.

Came hazy daylight and King Shabaka, sore and ashy, muzzy with sleep, saw Noi sitting cross-legged, finger-feeding herself stewed roots covered with sauce from a smooth-grained bowl. By her side lay his chalk.

"Good morning, King Shabaka."

"What's good about it?" He was a crocodile awakening, was the king.

"It's this," asked Noi, "that brings things to life?"

King Shabaka scratched the side of his neck. He stretched his legs to start blood circulating again, and nodded. "A gift from the wizards."

42

"It makes you the most powerful man in all Africa, King, if you can turn the fruits of Mind into Matter like *that!*" She snapped her fingers. "And though I'm no one to tell a mighty king his business, I think you should put this in the service of the Allmuseri—heal the sick, feed the poor. That sort of thing."

"You speak obscurely," said the king, although the truth was that he had earth wax clogging the cartilage in his ears this morning. "Explain what you mean."

"The Allmuseri are, will always be, a poor village." She became formal, like a wizard leaning on his wand, lecturing. "Our fields where the old women and small boys work are stingy. Our hunters return home empty-handed. There is never enough meat, or—or—or anything, O King."

"I shall draw it," Shabaka said. "Mountains of meat. No one shall go hungry."

"And when the chalk is gone?"

"I'll draw more chalk." He cackled. But when he tried to draw more chalk, nothing happened. "Always a catch to these things." Shabaka scowled and pursed his lips. "Poo!"

Noi continued, her nose twitching. "With the magic that remains, the Allmuseri could control lands and forests and rivers from the sea to the desert. They could increase in size, add colonies, King—are you listening? You could conquer the outlying cannibal

Wazimba, who from old have held a grudge against us—as fierce as the Hutu have for the Tutsi—and carve from a handful of scattered, starving villages a single empire."

She stopped, her flat stomach pumping in, out, and gently blew a bad poem in his ear:

> *Chiefs and kings all bend to age,*
> *Sneezed kicking to the afterworld;*
> *But those chieftains truly sage,*
> *Leave their tribes great treasure.*

"Terrible!" The king frowned. "You didn't rhyme. Only once! And then poorly!"

"I know," Noi said sadly. "We are all frail, King. All systems collapse."

Still piqued, for truly he liked poems that rhymed, the king reached into the hindmost corner of his mind and found his boyhood of futile hoeing, his time of scouring forests where he hunted for food and brought home—after tramping all day in fumets aged to dry ash—only a handful of speckled bird eggs. His people farmed maize and millet, *watoto* and *viazi*, storing it in the walls of their huts before they were plastered over, the way a swallow builds her nest; but lately the stores were slight and from the hole at each hut's bottom there trickled only gray powder. The king considered his chalk. Then the girl. Then his own ashy foot. "Yes," he said, "one must will goodness and prosperity for others."

In the seventeenth century, owing to the furious sketching of King Shabaka, through three days and nights, the villages of the Allmuseri ballooned until they covered the area between Setti-Carnuna in the north and Benguella in the south. His pen pushed his people inland as far as the upper Zambezi, and he relocated the capital at Banya. And never have you seen such a palisaded capital as this—there were, not mud huts, but suspended gardens, high white walls, storied palaces shaped from orichalc and bdellium, pools inlaid with gold, arenas for sport, paved streets down which merchant caravans clattered from all the Four Corners and, for King Shabaka and Queen Noi, lodgings heavily upholstered with luxury. True, all this looked—well, a little weird, like the sketch of a child who places two eyes on one side of a head, for the capital was filtered through King Shabaka's flagging imagination. It was like living inside the canvas of a Chagall. Painters do not put every hair on a goatskin, nor every vein in a leaf, so King Shabaka's capital had large pieces missing (the main road ended, along with Shabaka's wit, halfway through the city; decorative trees in the plaza appeared without bark, dogs without tails, trees without perspective). Yet and still, the capital was dreamlike, reality transmogrified; even if it was physically wrong, it was poetically right.

He drew Noi quick with child, and from her issued a boy as beautiful as his queen. Flowing out onto the ground, steaming like a boiled egg, for it was in the coolness of the night when Noi gave birth, the baby's legs were entangled in his stringy umbilicus. The midwife—Shabaka's sister—ululated twice (meaning, "It's a boy!"), and the king hurried into the room, scooped up his child, and roared in his loudest voice, "All praise to Allah!"

Shabaka buried the placenta in the Descendent's Nest, a hole in the floor by his child's bed, to keep the newborn baby in the house. This child, Shabaka knew, was enchanted. "See his eyes?" said the king to Noi. "Mine! See his mouth? Also mine! See his brow? Hah! *That* is his grandfather's ponderous brow!" The queen wondered, "Nothing from me?" Shabaka reconsidered, "He has your—eh—*grace.*" Above all else, King Shabaka loved his son, whom he named Asoka, after his own father. Long hours he spent tickling his ribs and asking—before Asoka could speak and only splashed playfully in language—"Will you be a credit to your ancestors?" Chirping, Asoka rolled his eyes and squeezed Shabaka's fingers. He clapped his hands when Shabaka drew for his pleasure miniature armies and camels, and a tiny court that came to life shouting, "Long live the prince!"

It came to pass that the home of the Allmuseri became known as the "Empire of the Congo." It bordered on the south what is now known as the city of Massammedes, and its population mushroomed, taking in Hottentots, Damara, Bechuana, Bastudo, and Zulu peoples. The capital buzzed with commerce, the cant of merchants, the whine of beggars pleading for leftovers from sacrificial offerings at the cemeteries. And it also fortuned that Shabaka, as the years passed, prospered; he was in a paradise of pleasure— Asoka grew up gentle, pious, and scholarly, the sort of boy who cried when he saw a dead bird, or covered his eyes when clan cattle were butchered; but he was gifted too with a quicksilver wit that outdid Shabaka's fey wizards. He would be a *hafiz* and *osuo* both, that Asoka, because at fifteen he was already acquainted with the arcane charms of the Ekpe cults in the Cameroons and the curious arts of the Konkombe tribes of the Oti Plain. Yes, the boy pleased Shabaka who, with the growth of his villages into a kingdom, found his days taken up more and more by meetings, hollow ceremonies, disputes with the impossible Wazimba (as he called them) who were buying rifles and rum from ghostlike mariners who prowled the west coast of Africa. Added to that, there was now not enough of his omnifix chalk left to draw your attention. Shabaka never quite got over his astonishment that it was gone. But, all in all, he was the wealthiest, the happiest, the most loved man in this, a Golden Age, of ancient Africa.

Well might we leave our king here, for these were happy times, at least until the morning Nduku appeared at his door.

"King," said Nduku, "I have hard news."

Shabaka braced himself, balling his fists. "Tell of it."

"You must stop the Wazimba. They buy goods from the colorless men who come in great ships, paying them in slaves—debtors from their tribe at first, but now we have reports that the Wazimba have raided other villages. If they are not stopped, they will come *here*."

Asoka, now eighteen, sat nearby studying a scroll. He looked up and, before his father could speak, said, "Let me meet them in counsel."

"No!" said Shabaka. "I will go—"

Nduku raised one hand, lowering his eyes at the same time. "King, I think the prince speaks well. You have angered the Wazimba more than once. But Asoka's manner is pleasing, his words persuasive. I

48

would trust him to lead a delegation, and if he is successful, he will return home a hero."

Not because he wanted to did Shabaka agree, but because he knew that someday his son would have to assume the duties of the throne. When Nduku left, he gave his son the silver-headed spear. He kissed his forehead, and said, "I would shield you forever from pain and suffering. I would keep you innocent, but if I did so, you would never grow strong enough to be a king."

The next morning Shabaka watched Asoka, two of his advisors, and twenty warriors leave the capital to convince the Wazimba to cease their trade in human flesh. Remembering his old hut, kept under constant guard inside his palace because he had a fetish feeling about the place, King Shabaka went thitherward, then sat alone in this dream theater amidst the malodorous images of all he had wished for and willed in his lifetime. These drawings, he reasoned, were his deeds— the icons of palaces, of prosperity, of pleasure—and they were now like crustaceans that he could not brush away; they were his children and his father simultaneously, more his father than the late Asoka, as if his every word, gesture, idea had been recorded on an enormous tablet, objectified, and unfurled before him like a merchant's tacky cloth, so that Shabaka, breathing unsteadily, fingers snarled in his linty beard, could hear (*click!*) an inexorable machinery (*click!*) grinding away between all his earlier cravings (*click!*) and this awful awareness of Asoka's absence. Whoever is wise and will observe these things will see that it was too late for King Shabaka to have such thoughts. That night he slept, keeled over against the wall in his old plastered hut.

And he never awoke properly again.

Late in the afternoon of the next day, he learned that his son's entourage had not reached its destination. Tribes living in the Congo Valley, sympathetic to the Wazimba, and eager for European weapons and whiskey, took Asoka's party prisoners, then delivered them to the Wazimba for sale. This news cut off Shabaka's wind. To sell a prince into bondage—it was the deepest of humiliations. The Wazimba knew that; it was their way of settling old scores. Shabaka plucked out his beard in handfuls and threw dust on his head. Then, meeting with his counsel, he declared war on the Wazimba and their allies. "Destroy them all," he ordered when reviewing his troops. "Leave not one Wazimba alive!"

Like Shabaka, the Allmuseri warriors had loved Asoka. They carried their anger—and the king's own—to the western tribes, and there they lost control, slaughtering 320 of the Damara, hunting down women and children and hacking them to pieces. They looted, they raped. In one Damara village they started to kill the elders, then asked for treasure. After they received all the Damara had, Shabaka's troops put them to death, singing and dancing while beating the elders with clubs. And as they continued this carnage, spreading from one tribe to the next, the rage among the outlying tribes redoubled, and the fighting drew closer to Shabaka's dream capital. "We have fallen too far now," he thought. His son was in shackles, nothing would change that. His people were propelled toward a disastrous end. Then the enemy—all gleaming teeth and spears—swept thunderously, like a harmattan wind, inside the high, white walls.

Their strategy, Shakaba learned later when he was chained and waiting to be sold, was to form a semicircle in the shape of a bull's horn, with sixty warriors at each tip, all armed with *assegai*—short spears, and strong oxhide shields half a man's height. They harried the streets of the city, butchering men and cattle both, and pushed on toward the palace. Along the side streets women huddled, knives raised above the heads of their children to save them from slavery among the Wazimba—or the foul-smelling sailors who waited at the barracoons on the coast. Toward the end, Shabaka was no longer a reluctant king but a warrior himself, beheading and skewering men when the Wazimba and Darama swarmed like an army of ants up the palace steps, until he collapsed, slicing the air with his spear and carrying away the arm of a man who'd struck him on his temple.

Conscious hours later, he found himself in a coffle, bound at his neck to thirty others, his queen among them, her flesh scarred and bloodied. Night and day, night and day, night and day they were marched to the factory town on the coast. When darkness fell his captors had their way with Noi until she went mad, suddenly leaping to her feet, broken, blathering insanely, and threw herself upon a spear. For a moment the King went mad too. Then something in him flimmered out; he felt nothing when they threw Noi's body into the brush. Nothing when the rifle-bearing Wazimba pushed him and the others on toward the fort. And nothing when the coffle reached the barracoon.

The king slept a sleep like a drugged stupor. When he awoke, a Wazimba guard said, "Soon it will be over, Shabaka. You are alone now, like a grain of maize in an empty gourd. In a little while you will be sold. But if the white men do not want one as old as you, then you will die. Best to make yourself ready for the earth to receive you."

He had, it's true, given no thought to this; he was not ready. Shabaka sat, his dark hands dangling between his legs. Hours melted away. Where, he wondered, had he erred? He had acted to end hunger, need, want, and—behold—each act of the ego engendered suffering. But too late these reflections, too late even his grief. He could hear them. They were coming for him. He struggled for breath. It was time. Shabaka, for whom life and death now had no difference, watched the Wazimba forcing his people outside the barracoon and into the sunlight; then he looked up as strange men from across the sea beckoned him to rise—men with faces like metal, and no lips, as far as he could tell—who suddenly burst into honey-white needles of fire and light.

He was squatting in his hut, staring stupidly at the unmarked wall. Outside he heard Mahdi and Kangabar arguing. Rubbing his grainy eyes, the king whispered, "Inshallah!" He pinched himself experimentally—there were no scars; he had never married Noi, raised a kingdom, or a son. There were no slavers, no war, just the afterglow of these appearances in his mind. And this hut in the hot afternoon?—he reserved judgment for just now on this hut. Shabaka called in his sorcerers.

"It is well?" they asked together.

"No!" He pegged his chalk stick at Mahdi, bouncing it off the hard bone of his forehead. "You wizards," he asked, "why is it you have never used this fabulous toy to advance yourselves?"

"You joke." Mahdi rubbed his forehead. "Why, it ill-befits a sober man to swell the world's agony by adding his own desires to it, King. He fares best if he has maximum concern for life, but minimum attachment." The sorcerer studied the chalk, and asked, "You did not like our gift, King?"

Shabaka said, "It has made a perfect fool out of me. It's on your lips, Mahdi, to say I do a fine job of that myself, but I shall never know for sure whether all I do is substance or shadow, or whether history is naught but the nightmarish dream of a sleeping god who hasn't digested his dinner." Shabaka shambled to the large jar in his hut and poured three bowls of zythum. By evening these three crinkly heads were heated, for zythum, a beer of Egyptian brew, is 90 percent alcohol; and they soon were sleeping—after pouring a little beer on the floor for Allah and ancestors—slumped together on the floor.

Executive Decision

Act as if the principle of thy action were to become by thy will a universal law of nature.

—Kant, *Fundamental Principles of the Metaphysic of Morals*

PUT SIMPLY, your task is impossible.

There are two names shortlisted for the position your company has advertised. These two have surfaced as the most appealing candidates after a six-month search that left you and your Seattle staff red eyed and exhausted after sifting through the files of more than eight hundred applicants and phoning dozens of references, some of them as far away as southern France and Osaka. You've met their spouses, their children. Read their personal statements. Called them back for second interviews. Probed into their after-hours interests, taken them to dinner, and now you, and you alone—as the grandson of the company's founder—must decide. Naturally, both are being wooed by other businesses and by government. If you delay the decision any longer, you will lose them to a competitor. So by nine A.M. tomorrow the six-figure job, with its benefits and stock options, must be awarded to either Claire Bennett or Eddie Childs, and the other given an apology.

It is the most troublesome decision of your life.

Imprimis: You are a man who, though quite radical in your youth, has come to see the wisdom in not rocking the boat overly much if advocacy means the ship might take on too much water, its hull give way, and its many passengers—employees, stockholders, and their families—disappear beneath the briny. If nothing else, a life in business has so instilled in you the value of prudence that even your closest friends from college remark on how dull and safe, portly and bald you've become since the days you marched arm in arm with civil rights workers through the streets of Cambridge. Yet and still, in your personal and professional affairs alike, you have always believed in fairness, though on some occasions precisely what *is* fair seems elusive. The question was so much clearer in the black-and-white time of youth. Not long after your father became ill and the company passed into your hands thirty years ago, you insisted in board meetings that the personnel department aggressively seek out blacks and women.

It was an outrageous thing to do in 1966, but then you were fresh out of Harvard, with a degree in philosophy (partly to spite your parents), having focused on epistemology, the problems of appearances versus reality; two arrests for demonstrating on campus, with the oratory of Martin Luther King Jr.—"Power at its best is love implementing the demands of justice; justice at its best is love correcting everything that stands against love"—still echoing in your ears. At first your only supporter was old Gladys McNeal, your father's personal secretary, factotum, and possibly his lover as well. She is your secretary now—a precise, never-married woman who could pass for actress Estelle Getty's sister, though Gladys won't talk about her age and has never uttered a word about her family. She'd called your fight to hire more minorities and women "brave." And eventually, the company acquiesced to your wishes, placing more blacks on the custodial staff and women in the secretarial pool in the late '60s and early '70s, and a sprinkling of both in middle management during the '80s.

Lately some of the black employees have been grumbling to you and Gladys about the absence of African Americans in the firm's administrative wing. (Gladys only nods when the subject comes up and looks away, knowing they're right.) You can see them at their desks through the glass walls that separate their tiny, cluttered workstations from your spacious chamber (with its carpeted floors and plaster-of-paris bust of Cicero) and those of your two chief executives, old friends whom to this very day you still affectionately call by their fraternity nicknames, Turk and Nips—it's dyspeptic, eccentric old Turk who's retiring due to poor health and whose position Bennett and Childs hope to fill.

Except for a black janitor, the top-floor office in your downtown building on Fifth and Pine is empty at ten P.M. You have stayed behind to review the candidates' qualifications and your notes one last time. Their files—thicker than the white pages for Wenatchee— are spread out on your desk beneath the glow of the handcrafted lamp given to you as a birthday gift from your wife, Emilie, a painter who could not resist this high-end item that translates Monet's *Water Lilies* into five hundred multicolored glass panels on its triangular shade. In the light of this lamp, you pore over these pages, looking for the one fact or feeling that might edge one of these candidates ahead of the other. To your great perplexity, both look equally qualified—or, if not exactly matched, what you see as deficiencies in one are balanced by a strength the other does not possess.

But except before the law, and in the eyes of God, are *any* two people truly equal?

Claire, you recall, was forthcoming and full of wonderfully funny stories during her first three-hour interview. She was a graduate of Boston University. Even before you, Turk, and Nips sat her down in the conference room, with its breathtaking view of snow-capped Mount Rainier in the background, the four of you were swapping stories about your undergraduate days and New England associates you had in common. It was as if you'd known her all your life. She felt at home in the Northwest, having grown up in Portland, where her parents sent her to Catlin Gabel, a private school dating back to 1870 and one of the best independent academies in the region. Her parents, both professionals, provided her with private tutors, a course in modeling when she was fourteen (afraid she was awkward and unlovely), and trips with her father to Barcelona, Paris, and Tokyo when his work required that he travel (her Japanese was flawless). Despite an early struggle with epilepsy, which she controlled with Klonopin, Claire graduated from college near the top of her class, accepted her first job with a firm in Chicago, and, after several early promotions, found herself positioned as the assistant to the company's CEO when disaster struck in the form of a class-action suit against the firm. That, she explained, taught her more than anything she'd learned in college. Claire put out fires, she controlled the damage, and learned firsthand the meaning of a saying she'd heard when traveling in the Far East: "In chaos there is also opportunity."

During her interview she was relaxed, laughed easily, and scored points when she said, "I see my *first* job as being the protection of the company." She was twenty-eight years old, six-feet-two in her heels, and wore her corn-colored hair to her shoulders. And did she have faults? Nips felt Claire had slightly more nose than she needed. And he noticed that rather than completely agreeing with the things he said, she prefaced her replies by saying, "Yes, but . . ." and "Oh, it's *more* than that, of course . . ." Furthermore, she had done her homework and was aware of the company's history, its strengths and weaknesses, and guided her interview to such an extent that it seemed *they,* not she, were being looked over and scrutinized. That Nips didn't enjoy. On the other hand, Turk liked it just fine.

Claire's husband, Bill, a shaggy, bearded, Old English sheepdog of a fellow with hair falling into his brown eyes, came along for her second interview; he was self-employed—a moderately successful sculptor ("conceptual artist" was the term he preferred)—and could relocate with no difficulty if she got the job. He'd surprised you when, after shambling into your office in a corduroy jacket and jeans, he shook your hand firmly (his palm was rough, toughened like that of a carpenter), then paused to look at the lamp, and nodded in approval. "Nice, that's a reproduction of Louis Comfort Tiffany's work, isn't it? The bronze patina on the base places the design somewhere in the twenties . . ."

That you hadn't known—the lamp's history—but you and Emilie were pretty sure of this: You liked the Bennetts. Emilie called them "people persons." And so they were. Their ten-year-old daughter, a bright, brown-skinned girl named Nadia, was Filipino—their own child, a boy, had died from SIDS—and Nadia was the first of two or three children the Bennetts hoped to adopt. If you hired Claire, you knew she would not only protect the interests of your business as if it were her own, but her family and yours might become the best of friends. Added to which, and perhaps most important of all, she would be the first woman to break through the company's "glass ceiling," which was definitely a plus in the present, gender-charged political climate.

But then there was Childs . . .

He was thirty-one, from a large Atlanta family—four boys, five girls—and the first member of his family to graduate from college (Morehouse) after serving in the navy. On the day of his interview he looked trim and fit in his three-piece suit: a dark-skinned man with close-cropped hair, a thin mustache like movie star David Niven's, and nails more neatly manicured than your own. When he answered a question, or a series of them put to him by Nips and Turk, Childs always turned to look directly at the person who'd asked it, never forgetting who'd originated the query. But unlike Claire, even when he appeared at ease, you saw that Childs never completely relaxed. In high school, he confessed, a white teacher told him that he'd never be college material and directed him toward a blue-collar trade. "That woke me up," Childs said. "He made me so mad I guess I've been fighting to prove him wrong since I was fifteen years old."

You saw in Childs the attitude of a man who believed nothing would ever come to him easily, that he had to work twice as hard as others to get half as far—and four times that to break even. And so he had. He'd made his own opportunities. His record showed he'd worked full-time as a nightwatchman while attending Morehouse, studying and saving and having, he said, no social life at all. After college, he returned to Atlanta and started his own business from scratch, one he later sold, but not before Childs paid off the mortgage on his parents' home, and put one of his siblings through school. He was actively involved in his church, the NAACP, and a community group dedicated to helping at-risk youth. His references included half a dozen names in Atlanta's city government and two black congressmen. He had nothing to say about the lamp on your desk, but what he and his wife, Leslie, an elementary school teacher, knew firsthand and through research about this country's marginalized history—the contributions from people of color—stunned you, Turk, and Nips into respectful yet nervous silence.

You listened carefully to what he said.

You learned that blacks suffered twice the unemployment rate of whites and earned only half as much (56 percent); that a decade ago they comprised 7 percent of professionals, 5 percent of managers, 8 percent of technicians, 11 percent of service workers, and 41 percent of domestic workers. There were, he told you, 620,912 black-owned businesses, but 47 percent of them had gross annual receipts of less than $5,000. For every 1,000 Arabs, 108 owned a business; for every 1,000 Asians, it was 96; for every 1,000 whites, 64, and for every 1,000 blacks, the number was 9. Worse, the typical black household had a net worth less than one-tenth that of white households. AIDS among black Americans was six times the rate it was for whites, and every four hours a young black male died from gunfire. Seventy percent of black children were born to single mothers; 57 percent were in fatherless homes, which was more than double the 21 percent for whites. This was the background of poverty and inequality Eddie and Leslie Childs had survived—a world in which black men in the early '90s accounted for half those murdered in America; they had less chance of reaching age sixty-five than men in Bangladesh. One out of three was in prison (the number was 827,440 in 1995) or on parole. It was a world where, as Childs put it, quoting Richard Pryor, justice was known simply as "just ice." Given these staggering obstacles, you are amazed this man is even alive.

Little wonder then that during his visit he never seemed to relax, or let his hair down, or get too comfortable. You, Turk, and Nips were not sure he would ever completely trust you or, for that matter, much of anything in this world. But despite his admiration for this couple, Turk had reservations about Childs. After dinner he'd asked the candidate over to his home to join your Friday-night poker game, and Childs politely declined, saying, "I would prefer not to. I don't play cards." He confessed, "My wife is always saying I'm not much of a fun person. All I do is work." Yes, he was formal, guarded, and, even after two interview sessions, opaque. He was—what word do you want?—"different." Sometimes you did not understand his humor. You certainly did not know his heart—*that* would come slowly, perhaps even painfully if you presumed too much about him, and it might be hard at first, a challenge, with you tripping lightly, walking on eggs around him until everyone in the office eased into familiarity. Was one candidate worth all that work? In his interview Childs outlined two strategies for improving diversity in personnel and ideas for better marketing the firm's product to minorities who, he emphasized, would be in the minority no longer after the coming millennium. Nips felt he was right, but naturally *he* would, being never satisfied with the way things were in the world (including the desk in his office, which he was forever rearranging and replacing). In the morning he was always a little dull, possibly hungover (for Nips still enjoyed visiting nightspots where he met, he said, people from numerous walks

of life); but as the day progressed, and he slowly
sobered, his disposition generally improved. The
country's demographics were changing, Nips said.
All you had to do was walk out your door to see that.
If the company hoped to survive into the twenty-first
century, a multiracial arrangement was needed. He
cast his vote categorically for Childs, and asked you
and Turk to do the same.

But Turk would not budge on Bennett.

"Why discuss this any further?" he said, after Bennett returned to Chicago and Childs to Atlanta.
Between the three of you, a bottle of scotch from the
bottom drawer of your filing cabinet was passed
around, Nips drinking from a paper cup, Turk from a
coffee mug imprinted with the insignia of the Sea-
hawks. He'd made his decision by seven P.M., but
Turk was notorious for being a morning person, and
you seldom trusted anything he said or did after
lunch when his vitality was low, his round face
flushed pink, his manner rude, and his judgments
often dubious. "Bennett will be good for the operation, especially overseas. As reliable, I believe, as old
Gladys. I think she can weather any crisis that comes
along, make us a lot of money, and keep the stockholders happy. That's all *I* need to know." He chuck-
led into his mug. "She's no Nicholas Leeson."

"Who?" you asked.

"The British kid who brought down Baring Brothers and Company. You remember, don't you? The company was two hundred and thirty-two years old. It helped finance the Napoleonic wars. Lord knows how it happened, but they made Leeson manager of their Singapore office, and he gambled that the Tokyo market would go up. Turns out, it went down, and eight hundred million of Baring's money with it." Turk laughed again, wickedly. "I *love* that story. Just shows you what can happen if you hire wrong."

"But," asked Nips, "does Bennett *deserve* the job more than Childs?"

Turk's face tightened in a frown. "How's that again—deserve, I heard you say? We have a job to offer, and it's ours to extend or withhold as we see fit. We may hire or fire the most qualified employee, as legal scholar Richard Epstein puts it, for good reason, bad reason, or no reason at all."

"And you think that's prudent?"

"I think it's practical, yes. And perfectly within our rights."

"You are not," pressed Nips, "concerned about discrimination?"

"Oh, pshaw! We *all* discriminate, Nips! Every moment of every day we choose one thing rather than another on the basis of our tastes, prejudices, and preferences. How *else* can we achieve life, liberty, and the pursuit of happiness? I remember that *you*, back in our school days, never deigned to direct your affections toward women taller than yourself or, for that matter, toward men. It's reasonable, I'm saying, to have likes and dislikes, and to act upon them, to prefer this over that because, for heaven's sake, no two things in nature are the same. Really, man, be realistic. The Japanese don't spend a moment agonizing over things like this, and look how they trumped us in the eighties! Preferential policies have weakened this nation's GNP. And just *how* is one to decide *whom* to prefer when not only blacks but Hispanics, Native Americans, and twenty-eight varieties of Asians are listed as preferred by the federal government?"

Nips listened patiently, as he always did when Turk, slightly in his cups, tilted toward the pomp and preachment of a Thrasymachus. He nodded in agreement. "Racial categories *do* cause a lot of confusion." For a few moments he said nothing, hoping, no doubt, that you and Turk would ponder the stories reported about whites with only a fraction of Mexican or Indian blood who invoked a distant minority in their family tree to qualify for the government's set-aside programs.

Then quietly, he asked, "Do you remember that class we took with John Rawls?"

"Vaguely, yes. I nearly flunked it. Had something to

do with the state being like a joint-stock company. A lot of Hobbes and Locke rehashed, if I recall it rightly."

"There was more to it than that. He said when justice is seen as fairness, men of unequal circumstances agree to share one another's fate. Social advantage and native endowment of any sort—whether they be inherited wealth, talent, beauty, or imagination—are undeserved. They are products of the arbitrariness of fortune. But Rawls did not say we must eradicate these inequities, only adjust them so the least favored benefit too. If the fortunate do not share, then the least advantaged have every right to break the social contract that has so miserably failed to serve their needs. They riot. They rebel. Without the cooperation of the least favored, the social order collapses for *everyone*."

"I remember you did well in that course—"

"Better than you because in my final paper, I argued that it is in the interest of the favored to redress the wrongs caused by slavery and a century of segregation."

"Wronged by *whom*? Nips, I can assure you *I* had nothing to do with it. All that happened before our time!"

"Then we have *no* greater social obligations?"

"My dear friend," Turk said, patting Nips on his knee, "making the monthly payroll on time so employees and their families are not unduly inconvenienced is, in my humble opinion, social obligation enough. I am for the candidate who puts *that* first."

"Be honest," said Nips, "you're just not comfortable with colored people, are you?"

"That's hardly fair! I can't *say,* because I don't know any!"

"Exactly my point."

They argued that way for most of the evening, through three bottles of whiskey, long after Gladys clicked off the lights in the outer office (she pretty much ran the place, knew where all the bodies were buried, and was always the first employee to arrive and the last to leave). Turk and Nips staggered out together, carrying their disagreement into the hallway and elevator, neither of them willing to support the other's candidate for the job.

It falls to you to break the tie.

Come midnight, you are still torn, divided within as if you were two people, or perhaps three. No question that these candidates are antinomies. But what, then, is the just decision? Could there be color-blind decisions in a country wracked by race? Or was Turk correct that it was not a question of racial justice at all? All night you have worried this question into mere words, a blur of sound signifying, it seems, nothing. And now it is too late to catch the last ferry home to

Whidbey Island. Emilie no doubt has already tucked the children in bed and turned in for the night. After taking off your suit coat, kicking off your shoes, pulling loose your tie and top button, you run water into the coffeemaker, then wearily plop down on the black leather sofa, rubbing your face with both hands. You spread the files on the coffee table, staring at them for another hour. A *black* man. A *white* woman. No. That was wrong. These empty signifiers had names, faces, specific histories that exploded sterile sociological categories and rendered both candidates ineffable and inexhaustible in their individuality. Their portfolios provided no clues whatsoever to their promise, or to unkeying the paradox of justice. Wearily, you push them away, close your eyes, and drift in and out of sleep until sunlight brightens the room and, below the office window, night's silence swells with the sound of morning traffic.

Gladys opens the outer door at eight A.M. Her key in the latch sends you hurrying in your stocking feet to the bathroom and closet adjacent to your chamber. After splashing water on your face and brushing your teeth with two fingers, you reach into the closet where you keep a few fresh shirts still encased in crackling plastic from the cleaners. This is where your father kept his extra shirts and ties. It's where you played sometimes as a child, hiding in the closet when he dictated letters to Gladys. Four decades ago she'd been heartbreakingly beautiful, a brunette with bee-stung lips and eyes so green, so light, you wondered if she could really see through them. That she was quiet yet gentle, always smiling ironically, as if she had a secret, never talked about herself, or her relations in New Orleans, or what she did away from the office only added an element of mystery to the gaps in what one knew personally about her. You suppose a man like your father could fill that with all manner of fantasies if his marriage was stale, his duties heavy, and he believed, rightly or wrongly, that her secrets could heal. Your mother was the one who'd told you these things, but not angrily, because she'd had several affairs of her own. In fact, she'd seemed as amused by the brevity of your father's only midlife fling as by his choice.

Around your throat the shirt's top button strains, a sign you're getting fatter at fifty-one. You're about to swear when something happens outside in your office that stops you cold. Someone is whistling a few bars from "Uptown Downbeat," an Ellington tune, one of your father's favorites. Walking to the bathroom's partly opened door, you see Gladys tidying up the files you left on the coffee table. Her hair, once obsidian and shiny, curls around her head in a cap of gray when she removes her rainbow-colored scarf. Believing herself to be alone in the office, she does a little dance step, snapping her fingers, shaking her hips, and for a flicker-flash instant she seems as young, as beautiful as Halle Berry.

Different.

Then she notices you, abruptly stops dancing, and, after composing herself—she is Estelle Getty again—steps to the window and opens the curtains, flooding the room with sunlight.

"You didn't spend the night here again, did you?" For years she's spoken like that, the way a doting godmother would. It takes you a moment to find your voice.

"Afraid so."

"Would you like me to put on some coffee?"

"Please."

You watch her leave, understanding only now why she looked away when the blacks in middle management complained that there were no Negroes in administration. How had Nips put it? Categories were chimerical. Mere constructs. When she comes back, carrying a carafe filled with water and a bag of Starbucks, you try not to stare or seem too confounded that Gladys is black. Or is she? By all appearances, she is as white as you.

"Gladys," you say, clearing your throat, "you met both Bennett and Childs. Which one would you feel best about hiring?"

She pauses, cupping the carafe in both hands. "Is this a trick question?"

"No, honestly, which one?"

"Well, I liked them both, but—"

"But what?"

"Oh, it's nothing, just that Mr. Childs reminds me of Mr. Turk when he was hired. Neither was very much at ease. And I know your father never approved of Mr. Turk. His references weren't that good, if I remember, or his grades, but he got the job because he was your friend and you insisted. You acted on his behalf, and that was all right." She smiles and you see Halle Berry again; then, as the muscles around her mouth relax, Estelle Getty. "These matters are never neutral, are they?"

"No . . . I'd forgotten. . . ."

"And people are not what they seem initially."

"No . . ."

"It takes time to know anyone."

"Yes, I guess it does."

"Will there be anything else?"

"Gladys, I'm not sure how to ask this. You and my father—"

"Yes, sir?" Her smile is disarming, as if she knows what you need to say. "He was a wonderful man, one I could trust. I miss him very much."

"So do I. You can trust me too."

"I know that. Thank you, sir."

She returns to making the coffee, then when it is done brings you a cup with two packets of sugar and one of Cremora. Sitting down on the chair beside your desk, both hands folded on her lap, she asks:

"Did you decide?"

You tell her you have, lifting the cup, sipping carefully so as not to scald your lips. Your secretary has always taken her lunches alone. You know why, but today you will ask her to join you and Nips at Etta's, near the Pike Place Market.

"Shall I ring that person for you?"

"I think so, it must be eleven in Atlanta by now."

Better Than Counting Sheep

Although it embarrasses me to talk about my problems, I feel I have a responsibility to share with others the specific nightmare that took hold of my life one month ago, to share the condition I tried to keep secret but which was so obvious to everyone— especially to my colleagues and students in the Classics Department—to share the *curse*, if I may call it that, which began during the first week of classes this fall at the university, and how I discovered a cure.

Forgive me if I seem a bit evasive. My gift is not

for gab but is instead for solitary research, and it's not in my nature to talk overly much about myself. In fact, I've always dreaded being the center of attention, especially at professional conferences, where the thought of delivering a paper, with all those eyes grabbing at me, only magnified the shyness I've suffered from since I was a child. On the whole, and in general, I'm happiest when I'm quietly absorbed in study or solving an arcane puzzle of scholarship. So yes, it's true: I've always been a rather fubsy, bespeckled man with Chesterfieldian manners and more than a little resemblance to the late actor Burgess Meredith, or so my colleagues tell me, and for three decades my life has consisted of shuffling back and forth between my classes on Plato and my carrel at Suzzalo Library—lost in the campus crowd as I usually am and prefer to be—then returning to my one-bedroom apartment on Queen Anne Hill, crammed ceiling to floor with books, where each evening I fix myself a simple bachelor's dinner and, while relaxing in my pajamas and slippers, study the newspaper or a few journals like *Arion* and *Hellas* (to which I contribute) through my large, round reading glasses, and then around midnight I at last turn in.

Here is where the problem began.

The long and short of it is that I could fall asleep easily enough, but only for a short time. After only two hours I was suddenly wide awake, staring into the darkness, as alert as if I'd drunk five cups of Starbucks coffee in a row, my mind chewing on all sorts of cultural and scientific conundrums—for example, I could not stop thinking about the Poincare Conjecture (the Clay Mathematics Institute will pay anyone $1 million if they solve it). I kept brooding on questions like, What does it mean that water has been discovered on Mars? Will the Human Genome Project lead to genetic engineering? What *are* dolphins *saying* to each other with all those clicks, whistles, barks, and screeches? Were they talking about us? Will the e-book replace paperback novels? And just what *are* the ingredients that make the gooey blob inside Lava Lamps bubble and burble the way it does?

These sibyline mysteries, as you might guess, can keep an old-fashioned humanist awake until daybreak, pacing the floor and pulling at his hair, and that is exactly what I did. Without sleep, I felt like a fried egg all during my morning and afternoon seminars. I drumbled home to my apartment in a daze. I fell asleep—yes—but for only two hours once again. This purgatory went on for thirty days.

By the eighth day I was desperate. There were puffy, dark pouches under my eyes. My sleep-deprived brain felt like one long smear along the inside of my skull. Yet I had not *truly* been awake for that past week. Time felt fibrous, each moment unlocked from the next. Sounds, as they came to me, were faint, yeasting in the distance, a pâté of noises that blurred into an indistinguishable hum. The world looked as if it shimmered behind a curtain of heat. Insomnia, as others have pointed out, is a kind of waking limbo, a dreamlike realm *between* the beta-wave state of wakefulness and the theta-wave state of deep sleep. And it is well-known, especially to men and women of science, that if one does not sleep, one will go mad. We need REMs—Rapid Eye Movements—during deep sleep for the brain's electrical discharge of energy.

Knowing all this only magnified my fears—and, therefore, my enervating inability to sleep. My physician sympathized, as doctors are supposed to do, and prescribed a new sleeping pill, Ambien, but I went through two bottles of that stuff, and I was still sleepless in Seattle. I tried drinking warm milk because it contained the amino acid tryptophan, which the body uses to manufacture serotonin, which plays a role in regulating sleep, but again, nothing! I tried alcohol, but that just left me hungover *and* awake. I went to the gymnasium on campus and rode the stationary bike for three hours, lifted weights, and did one hundred push-ups, all of which left my body feeling like a construction site, but still I didn't sleep. I tried crossword puzzles and watching the History Channel until five A.M. I tried reading novels by Dean Koontz and Jacqueline Susann and Tom Clancy. I prayed, I took a hot bath, then began practicing yoga and transcendental meditation. I tried acupuncture. At night, in bed, I listened to a device I ordered from a catalog, a little wooden box that played the sound of waterfalls and the sweep of ocean waves, like a lullaby, but all that running water just made me want to get up and go to the bathroom to relieve my bladder. I even took up the study of Sanskrit, hoping against all hope that all those declensions and the five hundred case endings for masculine, feminine and neuter nouns would *surely* put me to sleep. But with Sanskrit I discovered a language so lovely that I was thrilled to learn that in this ancient, melic tongue, the words for "ocean" were *samudra* and *udadhi*, the words for "moon" were *chandra* and *indu*, and so I found myself so fascinated and absorbed I was still awake at dawn (*ushasa*, in Sanskrit).

After four weeks there seemed no cure for my affliction. I became resigned to the fact that my brain would always feel baked, that during my classes I would be groggy and the edges of my mind blurred, with the whole world seeming to tilt on its axis. I was in that state as I left my afternoon seminar on the thirtieth day of this misery, and it was on the second floor of Padelford Hall that I ran into my chairman, who was almost sprinting toward the conference room behind me.

"Her-*win*!" he said. (My name is Herwin Throckmorton.) "You're just in time! There's an emergency we *have* to discuss!"

He took me by my arm, steering me into the crowded conference room, where all my colleagues were gathered. It was a windowless room, I should point out, and there were only two seats left at the head of the long conference table. My chairman took one while I collapsed in the other. All my colleagues stared at me in shock, because it was well-known that I *never* went to faculty meetings, not if I could avoid them. But all of that, remarkably, was about to change.

My chairman unpacked his briefcase, pulling out official-looking papers. He called the meeting to order, explaining the latest crisis that had befallen our little department, and I wish to heaven I could tell you exactly what that new crisis was, but I cannot because we have at least three crises every quarter, and as soon as his assistant began reviewing the minutes of the *last* meeting, and my chairman launched into a summary of the department's budget and future plans, adding (as he always does) a tirade against the administrators who favored the hard sciences over the struggling humanities and the arts, which explained why we classical scholars were perpetually overworked and under-appreciated and why all our salaries were so abysmally low—as he launched into this familiar jeremiad, I found myself helplessly drifting in and out of that hot, oxygen-depleted room, catching one of his phrases here and there, then I passed through another wave of warm torpidity that washed over me wonderfully, dropping me down—ever down—a deep well (*cupa* in Sanskrit) of blissful unconsciousness, and just before I started to snore loudly (for five straight hours, my colleagues and the school janitor later told me), sleeping like a whale on the surface of the sea, I was indeed thankful to the powers that be for the soporific qualities of faculty meetings, and I knew—as I've known nothing else in my life—that from that moment forward, I would happily attend *every* boring business meeting for the rest of the year, and perhaps the rest of my life, simply in order to catch up on my sleep.

The Queen and the Philosopher

In 1649, Queen Christina of Sweden became interested in Descartes' work and prevailed upon him to come to Stockholm. This Scandinavian sovereign was a true renaissance character. Strong-willed and vigorous, she insisted that Descartes should teach her philosophy at five in the morning. This unphilosophic hour of rising at dead of night in a Swedish winter was more than Descartes could endure. He took ill and died in February 1650.

—Bertrand Russell,
The Wisdom of the West

YEARS AND YEARS agone I cautioned Meister Descartes about this dangerous young woman, the notorious Queen Christina, and, to his credit, he *did* heed my monitions the first time she sent one of her warships to fetch him to Sweden.* I mean, didn't he have enough troubles already? She wanted him to serve as her personal tutor in philosophy and mathematics. At the time we were living not too uncomfortably in Holland on an estate twenty miles north of Amsterdam. The master enjoyed performing his daily meditations in a study shaped like an octagon, and this overlooked a beautiful garden, the sight of which brought him a feeling of serenity—his meditations were, of course, always in the afternoons or evenings, because all his life he was in the habit of sleeping ten hours a day and never rising before noon. I, Gustav Schulter, his valet and secretary who knew my place in this world and was not likely to rise above it, was at Descartes' side when he politely declined Queen Christina's invitation to join her court. He gave the admiral of her warship a letter that praised the queen's beauty, her likeness to God, and he requested, regretfully,

---

*Significant biographical research in this story is drawn from Paul Strathern's superb little book, *Descartes in 90 Minutes* (Chicago: Ivan R. Dee, 1996).

that she forgive his inability at the moment to bask "in the sunbeams of her glorious presence."

If matters had ended there—if, for example, she had given up and set her sights instead on Francis Bacon or Galileo as trophies to be installed in the Swedish court for her amusement—all would have gone well, I believe, for the father of modern philosophy. However, twenty-two-year-old Christina was not to be denied. She sent a *second* ship from Sweden to bring her Descartes. Was this a highborn hijacking? An aristocratic body snatching? Call his capture what you will. My master, whose cup-hilt rapier once held at bay a gang of buccaneers—devils, one and all—intent upon robbing him of his fine garments, was defeated. One does not decline when royalty comes calling *twice*. So in October 1649, and after our friends said, "Goodbye and Godspeed," we began our exodus and exile from Holland, sailing for Stockholm—and straight into the most nightmarish cautionary tale (or *conte philosophique*) any metaphysician has ever known.

During our passage through the Baltic Sea, as our vessel swung lazily from side to side on the gray-slick waters, I very much wondered at his acquiescence to the whim of a willful monarch said to prefer her art collection to the welfare of her people. He was fifty-three that fall, twice her age, and though he still cut a sartorial, if strange, figure, you would not have

guessed from his guise the depths of his genius. In
stature he was small, with a gigantic head and more
than enough Gallic nose for two or three Parisians. If
you squinted, blurring his image a bit, he looked rather
like a magpie or a crow that decided one day to become
a man, but only got halfway. His voice was frail. As his
valet I knew him to be a good Catholic, a solitary, a self-
ish, an unmarried, and at times a highly eccentric man.
For example, he told me that on November 11, 1619,
he took to living inside a stove during an especially
harsh winter in Bavaria. But it was there—inside his
stove (or, as some claim, his stove-heated room)—that
he experienced a Platonic vision of the world portrayed
entirely in terms of the eternal beauty of mathematics. This mystical moment directed him inward, to his
suspending all his beliefs and systematically doubting
the existence of *every*thing—the world, God, his per-
ceptions—until he could find something so apodictic
and certain that even the Almighty, if he was an Evil
Deceiver, could not fool him about it. That certainty,
said my master, was the thinking self. His *cogito ergo
sum*—"I think, therefore I am"—became the most oft-
quoted sentence in (and the foundation of) Western
philosophy in our time, and from this single brick of
rationalism he rebuilt a mechanistic world, dividing it
into mind substances (*res cogitans*) and physical substances (*res extentias*), with a benevolent God standing

above it all, ensuring that the innate ideas he had implanted within us were true. His bifurcation of phenomena into Mind and Matter—into two separate "truths," as it were—was a politically shrewd compromise that left men of science free to explore things material, and men of the cloth free to hold forth on things *im*material, such as the soul, that Ghost in the Machine. (For example, in the master's philosophy, animals were merely machines controlled by external stimuli.) So yes, Descartes carved out a space in the ruins of medieval scholasticism for science to progress. Just the same, his *Meditations,* and his methods, still ignited controversy across the European continent. The Jesuits sensed that his systematic doubt would be their undoing. The president of Holland's most esteemed university condemned him as an atheist, and the Calvinists in the Netherlands accused him of heresy. I know little of these things, being only a humble valet, but I gathered that once you become famous, you can count on getting famous problems.

Notwithstanding his misgivings about Queen Christina, and moving to Sweden, I suspect he saw her offer in terms of his present troubles with the Church. She hoped the founder of analytic geometry, the creator of Cartesian coordinates, and the man who revolutionized optics by discovering the law of refraction would help her create in her country an academy of sciences that would rival anything in Paris. Christina planned to make him a naturalized Swedish citizen, bring him into the Swedish aristocracy, and give him an estate on German lands she had conquered. Unless I am beguiled by the master's Evil Deceiver, Descartes saw her proposal as almost too good to be true—she would, he imagined, save him from his enemies in the Church, and among other philosophers, who were amplifying their opposition to his ideas.

As things turned out, her proposal—like so many in this life—*was* too good to be true. Descartes once said he wrote his *Meditations* in an autobiographical style to make it accessible to women. Maybe he succeeded too well, for Queen Christina not only understood his philosophical musings, but she saw his blunders as well. In every respect she was magnific. Before Christina was born astrologers predicted she would be a boy, and at first everyone thought King Gustavus Adolphus did have a son because she came into the world with a caul covering her pelvis. Forasmuch as the king had no male heirs, her father ordered that Christina was to be raised and trained as a prince. She was easily the homeliest woman in all Christiandom and stood only five feet tall in her slippers. But this "Queen of Sweden, of the Goths, and the Wends" was vigorously athletic, tough as an armadillo, disciplined, crisp, and efficient, and spent twelve hours a day, six days a week at sports and her studies. Christina wrote and spoke five languages. Her favorite activities were riding and hunting bears. She never slept more than five hours a night. Like a well-trained soldier, she took little food, was contemptuous of extremes of heat and cold, and expected the same Spartan behavior from everyone around her. Not too surprisingly, she refused to marry, and it was rumored that she liked girls, specifically a young countess named Ebba Sparre, new to her court. "It is necessary to try to *surpass* one's self always," Christina was fond of saying. "This occupation ought to last as long as life." She also was famous for saying, "I myself find it much less difficult to strangle a man than to fear him."

I must confess that I, Gustav, not being a bold man, *did* fear this galloping *Ubermensch* of a queen. There was no question that Descartes was fond of her. In public conversations he praised her for being "the Philosopher Queen," and in private talks with me called her his "Viking Amazon"; she called *him* whatever she pleased.

On the day we arrived he was feasted with smorgasbord, schnapps, and glögg, and lavishly honored by her court, as was appropriate for a luminary such as himself. But then Christina dropped her first royal slipper. After granting him permission to see her only twice, she informed Descartes that she was busy with affairs of state and could not begin her lessons with him for at least six weeks. During that time, she said, he should productively occupy himself with writing a ballet in verse to commemorate her role in the Peace of Westphalia, which concluded the Thirty Years' War. Besides all this, she ordered him to compose a comedy in five acts, and draw up the statutes for a Swedish Academy of Arts and Sciences.

So, as I say, Descartes was not happy about this delay, but it couldn't be helped. To these time-wasting chores he dutifully applied himself as, saints preserve us, a cold, dark winter set in—the worst winter in sixty years—and turned Stockholm into a hyperborean cavern buried beneath a hundred kinds of snow, with ice forming in your hair if you were outside for but a few moments. The temperature fell well below zero. My master seemed to keep a cold. "By heaven, Gustav, my old friend," he said through clogged-up sinuses, "it seems to me that men's thoughts freeze here during the winter, just as does the water. Our brains *are*, you know, eighty percent liquid."

Anon, he came to see how cruel, how unforgiving was this northern climate. And also how wickedly devious Queen Christina could be when after six weeks she dropped her *second* royal slipper. She knew—as *every*one knew—that erenow Descartes slept until noon. Christina, on the other hand, was out of bed each day at four A.M. She wanted her lessons in philosophy and mathematics three times a week at the wee hour of five A.M. in the unheated library of her royal palace, with all the windows thrown open. Perhaps she felt her regimen of defying refrigeration, of being indifferent to discomfort, would help Descartes to "surpass himself always."

In truth, it had the opposite effect, and for the first time I began to suspect she was in league with the Devil. For two difficult weeks I helped the master out of bed at three A.M. It was, I must say, like trying to bring Lazarus back to life. I filled his shivering, sleep-deprived body with hot tea; I helped him out of his nightshirt and into his black coat, knee breeches, and thick woolen scarf. I guided Descartes through his elaborate French toiletries, then I drove him in a sleigh over the frost-surfaced, sleety ground thither to her castle, the air raw and stinging my lungs, and with him all the while sneezing and coughing and shivering as if he might shake himself apart.

There, just outside her frigid, windswept library lined on all sides with books, Descartes trembled. As the queen bade him enter, he shook off a sudden wave of drowsiness and his cold-stiffened fingers brought forth from his valise the pages of the statutes he'd written for her academy. In a voice still phlegmed by sleep, he said, "Your Highness, I hope these pages will please you."

"For your sake, I hope they do." Christina was lively, even playful at this godforsaken, gelid hour. Spread out on a long table before the queen were my master's books. A thin wind through the windows changed the room's pressure and all at once my left ear felt stopped up, my right had a ringing sound, and my toes felt like knots of wood. So please don't think poorly of me if my memory of this tutorial appears sketchy. Reaching back, I do remember her saying, "But there is something in your published writing that troubles me. You say that Mind and Matter are separate substances. But if my soul *wills* my left hand to rise"—as she said this Christina gave the air a swipe with the back of her hand—"it remains a mystery how the immaterial will can affect my material body."

Descartes' teeth chattered loudly. His steamy breath rolled out: "Your Majesty, it is my belief that the interaction of the soul and body occurs in the pineal gland, where—"

"Just a moment! Don't speak! *Stop!*"

The master pulled up short, his mouth snapping shut, and he let his gaze fall to where his feet felt cemented to the floor.

"Do you have *evidence* for this?" she asked.

"Well, not exactly . . ."

"Oh, pooh, then the idea is preposterous, isn't it?" Christina put her head back. "Why *there*? Why not in the kidneys? Or the stomach?"

No one had pointed out this problem to him until now, or at least not so forcefully. My master, in a mental fog, tried to answer; his mouth opened, but no sound was forthcoming, as if his thoughts had glaciated. I suffer you then to see this almost Siberian chamber in the middle of a Scandinavian winter as the inner circle of a Hell perfectly designed for slugabed René Descartes.

The Ice Queen smiled and sat back in her chair.

"Do you see my problem, dear? For want of a better phrase, I would call it a 'mind-body problem,' an unnecessary and silly dualism that *you've* created. And this theory of yours about animals being machines is a delicious piece of sophistry! My goodness, I never saw my *clock* making babies!"

Particles of snow drifted inside and settled on Descartes' books. Weaving from the paralytic chill, he blew hot breath into his hands until they heated a little, briefly defrosting himself long enough to say, "Your Highness, *every*thing I've written logically follows if you begin, as I did, with systematic doubt."

The queen rolled her head to the left, and raised

her right eyebrow. "But your *Meditations* are not at all systematic, and they are fatally flawed."

His voice slipped a scale. "They *are*?"

"Forgive me if I speak frankly, for I'm not the world-famous philosopher *you* are, but I boast a knowledge of many things, as every monarch should." She looked at him steadily, as she might a bear she had just cornered. "If you stop doubting everything when you reach your own thoughts of doubt, you *can't* just say, 'I think, therefore I am,' because all you can be truly *certain* of at that moment is that thought is going on. You've assumed and added a self, an *I*, that is not *given*—only presupposed—in that experience."

My master looked sacked and empty. His frostbitten limbs were stiff and mechanical, like the fantastic animals that populated his philosophy. "I think . . . I need more time . . . to consider this, Your Majesty."

"*Do* consider, it," she said. "Be advised that I would like a good answer when we meet again two days from now."

That next tutorial was not destined to be. The master never completely thawed. He came down with pneumonia, and seven days after his lesson with the queen, he first slipped into delirium, then on February 11, 1650, a coma from which he never emerged. His body was buried near the queen's estate in a small Catholic cemetery for unbaptized children. And how did I, Gustav, feel now that my master was gone? Who-ever is wise must conclude that every original thinker would do well to fear too much attention from the High and Mighty. I wanted to go home and cry into my wife's bosom for a while. But I didn't have a wife. Eventually, I did return to Germany, with Christina's unanswered questions still shimmering in my mind. And even now, late at night when I try unsuccessfully to sleep, and look back on those bone-chilling months, I find myself unable to decide if the queen was a brief footnote in Meister Descartes' history, or if he, poor soul, was simply a footnote in hers.

Kwoon

DAVID LEWIS's martial-arts *kwoon* was in a South Side Chicago neighborhood so rough he nearly had to fight to reach the door. Previously, it had been a dry cleaner's, then a small Thai restaurant, and although he Lysol-scrubbed the buckled linoleum floors and burned jade incense* for the Buddha before each class, the studio was a blend of pungent odors, the smell of starched shirts and the tang of cinnamon pastries riding alongside the sharp smell of male sweat from nightly workouts. For five months David had bivouacked on the backroom floor after his students left, not minding the clank of presses from the print shop next door, the noisy garage across the street or even the two-grand bank loan needed to renovate three rooms with low ceilings and leaky pipes overhead. This was his place, earned after ten years of training in San Francisco and his promotion to the hard-won title of *sifu*.

As his customers grunted through Tuesday-night warm-up exercises, then drills with Elizabeth, his senior student (she'd been a dancer and still had the elasticity of Gumby), David stood off to one side to watch, feeling the force of their *kiais* vibrate in the cavity of his chest, interrupting them only to correct a student's stance. On the whole his students were a hopeless bunch, a Franciscan test of his patience. Some came to class on drugs; one, Wendell Miller, a retired cook trying to recapture his youth, was the obligatory senior citizen; a few were high school dropouts, orange-haired punks who played in rock bands with names like Plastic Anus. But David did not despair. He believed he was duty bound to lead them, like the Pied Piper, from Sylvester Stallone movies to a real understanding of the martial arts as a way that prepared the young, through discipline and large doses of humility, to be of use to themselves and others. Accordingly, his sheet of rules said no high school student could be promoted unless he kept a B average, and no dropouts were allowed through the door until they signed up for their GED exam; if they got straight A's, he took them to dinner. Anyone caught fighting outside his school was suspended. David had been something of a punk himself a decade earlier, pushing nose candy in Palo Alto, living on barbiturates and beer before his own teacher helped him see, to David's surprise, that in his spirit he had resources greater than anything in the world outside. The master's picture was just inside the door, so all could bow to him when they entered David's school. Spreading the style was his rationale for moving to the Midwest, but the hidden agenda, David believed, was an inward training that would make the need for conflict fall away like a chrysalis. If nothing else, he could make their workouts so tiring none of his students would have any energy left for getting into trouble.

Except, he thought, for Ed Morgan.

He was an older man, maybe forty, with a bald spot and razor burns that ran from just below his ears to his throat. This was his second night at the studio, but David realized Morgan knew the calisthenics routine and basic punching drills cold. He'd been in other schools. Any fool could see that, which meant the new student had lied on his application about having no formal training. Unlike David's regular students, who wore the traditional white Chinese T-shirt and black trousers, Morgan had changed into a butternut running suit with black stripes on the sleeves and pants legs. David had told him to buy a uniform the week before, during his brief interview. Morgan refused. And David dropped the matter, noticing that Morgan had pecs and forearms like Popeye. His triceps could have been lifted right off Marvin Hagler. He was thick as a tree, even top-heavy, in David's opinion, and he stood half a head taller than the other students. He didn't *have* a suit to fit Morgan. And Morgan moved so fluidly that David caught himself frowning, a little frightened, for it was as though the properties of water and rock had come together in one creature. Then he snapped himself back, laughed at his silliness, looked at the clock—only half an hour of class remained—then clapped his hands loudly. He popped his fingers on his left hand, then his right, as his students, eager for his advice, turned to face him.

"We should do a little sparring now. Pair up with somebody your size. Elizabeth, you work with the new students."

"*Sifu?*"

It was Ed Morgan.

David paused, both lips pressed together.

"If you don't mind, I'd like to spar with you."

One of David's younger students, Toughie, a Filipino boy with a falcon emblazoned on his arm, elbowed his partner, who wore his hair in a stiff Mohawk, and both said, "Uh-oh." David felt his body flush hot, sweat suddenly on his palms like a sprinkling of saltwater, though there was no whiff of a challenge, no disrespect in Morgan's voice. His speech, in fact, was as soft and gently syllabled as a singer's. David tried to laugh:

"You sure you want to try me?"

"Please." Morgan bowed his head, which might have seemed self-effacing had he not been so tall and still looking down at David's crown. "It would be a privilege."

Rather than spar, his students scrambled back, nearly falling over themselves to form a circle, as if to ring two gunfighters from opposite ends of town. David kept the slightest of smiles on his lips, even when his mouth tired, to give the impression of masterful indifference—he was, after all, *sifu* here, wasn't he? A little sparring would do him good. Wouldn't he? Especially with a man the size of Morgan. Loosen him up, so to speak.

He flipped his red sash behind him and stepped lower into a cat stance, his weight on his rear leg, his lead foot light and lifted slightly, ready to whip forward when Morgan moved into range.

Morgan was not so obliging. He circled left, away

from David's lead leg, then did a half step of broken rhythm to confuse David's sense of distance, and then, before he could change stances, flicked a jab at David's jaw. If his students were surprised, David didn't know, for the room fell away instantly, dissolving as his adrenaline rose and his concentration closed out everything but Morgan—he always needed to get hit once before he got serious—and only he and the other existed, both in motion but pulled out of time, the moment flicker-ish, fibrous, and strangely two-dimensional, yet all too familiar to fighters, perhaps to men falling from heights, to motorists microseconds before a head-on collision, these minutes a spinning mosaic of crescent kicks, back fists and flurry punches that, on David's side, failed. All his techniques fell short of Morgan, who, like a shadow—or Mephistopheles—simply dematerialized before they arrived.

The older man shifted from boxing to *wu*-style *t'ai chi ch'uan*. From this he flowed into *pa kua*, then Korean karate: style after style, a blending of a dozen cultures and histories in one blink of an eye after another. With one move he tore away David's sash. Then he called out each move in Mandarin as he dropped it on David, bomb after bomb, as if this were only an exhibition exercise.

On David's face blossoms of blood opened like orchids. He knew he was being hurt; two ribs felt broken, but he wasn't sure. He thanked God for endorphins—a body's natural painkiller. He'd not touched Morgan once. Outclassed as he was, all he could do was ward him off, stay out of his way—then not even that when a fist the size of a cantaloupe crashed straight down, driving David to the floor, his ears ringing then, his legs outstretched, like a doll's. He wanted to stay down forever but sprang to his feet, sweat stinging his eyes, to salvage one scrap of dignity. He found himself facing the wrong way. Morgan was behind him, his hands on his hips, his head thrown back. Two of David's students laughed.

It was Elizabeth who pressed her sweat-moistened towel under David's bloody nose. Morgan's feet came together. He wasn't even winded. "Thank you, *Sifu*." Mockery, David thought, but his head banged too badly to be sure. The room was still behind heat waves, though sounds were coming back, and now he could distinguish one student from another. His sense of clock time returned. He said, "You're a good fighter, Ed."

Toughie whispered, "No shit, *bwana*."

The room suddenly leaned vertiginously to David's left; he bent his knees a little to steady his balance. "But you're still a beginner in this system." Weakly, he lifted his hand, then let it fall. "Go on with class. Elizabeth, give everybody a new lesson."

"David, I think class is over now."

Over? He thought he knew what that meant. "I guess so. Bow to the master."

His students bowed to the portrait of the school's founder.

"Now to each other." Again, they bowed, but this time to Morgan.

"Class dismissed."

Some of his students were whooping, slapping Morgan on his back as they made their way to the hallway in back to change. Elizabeth, the only female, stayed behind to let them shower and dress. Both she and the youngest student, Mark, a middle school boy with skin as smooth and pale as a girl's, looked bewildered, uncertain as to what this drubbing meant.

David limped back to his office, which also was his bedroom, separated from the main room by only a curtain. There, he kept equipment: free weights, a heavy bag on which he'd taped a snapshot of himself—for who else did he need to conquer?—and the rowing machine Elizabeth avoided, calling it Instant Abortion. He sat down for a few seconds at his unvarnished kneehole desk bought cheap at a Salvation Army outlet, then rolled onto the floor, wondering what he'd done wrong. Would another *sifu*, more seasoned, simply have refused to spar with a self-styled beginner?

After a few minutes he heard them leaving, a couple of students begging Morgan to teach them, and really, this was too much to bear. David, holding his side, his head pulled in, limped back out. "Ed," he coughed, then recovered. "Can I talk to you?"

Morgan checked his watch, a diamond-studded thing that doubled as a stopwatch and a thermometer, and probably even monitored his pulse. Half its cost would pay the studio's rent for a year. He dressed well, David saw. Like a retired champion, everything tailored, nothing off the rack. "I've got an appointment, *Sifu*. Maybe later, okay?"

A little dazed, David, swallowing the rest of what he wanted to say, gave a headshake. "Okay."

Just before the door slammed, he heard another boy say, "Lewis ain't no fighter, man. He's a dancer." He lay down again in his office, too sore to shower, every muscle tender, strung tight as catgut, searching with the tip of his tongue for broken teeth.

As he was stuffing toilet paper into his right nostril to stop the bleeding, Elizabeth, dressed now in high boots and a baggy coat and slacks, stepped behind the curtain. She'd replaced her contacts with owl-frame glasses that made her look spinsterish. "I'm sorry—he was wrong to do that."

"You mean win?"

"It wasn't supposed to be a real fight! He tricked

you. Anyone can score, like he did, if they throw out all the rules."

"Tell him that." Wincing, he rubbed his shoulder. "Do you think anybody will come back on Thursday?" She did not answer. "Do you think I should close the school?" David laughed, bleakly. "Or just leave town?"

"David, you're a good teacher. A *sifu* doesn't always have to win, does he? It's not about winning, is it?"

No sooner had she said this than the answer rose between them. Could you be a doctor whose every patient died? A credible mathematician who couldn't count? By the way the world and, more important, his students reckoned things, he was a fraud. Elizabeth hitched the strap on her workout bag, which was big enough for both of them to climb into, higher on her shoulder. "Do you want me to stick around?"

"No."

"You going to put something on that eye?"

Through the eye Morgan hadn't closed, she looked flattened, like a coin, her skin flushed and her hair faintly damp after a workout, so lovely David wanted to fall against her, blend with her—disappear. Only, it would hurt now to touch or be touched. And, unlike some teachers he knew, his policy was to take whatever he felt for a student—the erotic electricity that sometimes arose—and transform it into harder teaching, more time spent on giving them their money's worth. Besides, he was always broke; his street clothes were old enough to be in elementary school: a thirty-year-old man no better educated than Mark or Toughie, who'd concentrated on shop in high school. Elizabeth was another story: a working mother, a secretary on the staff at the University of Illinois at Chicago, surrounded all day by professors who looked young enough to be graduate students. A job as sweet as this, from David's level, seemed high-toned and secure. What could he offer Elizabeth? Anyway, this might be the last night he saw her, if she left with the others, and who could blame her? He studied her hair, how it fell onyx black and abundant, like some kind of blessing over and under her collar, which forced Elizabeth into the unconscious habit of tilting her head just so and flicking it back with her fingers, a gesture of such natural grace it made his chest ache. She was so much lovelier than she knew. To his surprise a line from *Psalms* came to him: "I will praise thee, for I am fearfully and wonderfully made." Whoever wrote that, he thought, meant it for her.

He looked away. "Go on home."

"We're having class on Thursday?"

"You paid until the end of the month, didn't you?"

"I paid for six months, remember?"

He did—she was, literally, the one who kept the light bill paid. "Then we'll have class."

All that night and half the next day, David stayed horizontal, hating Morgan. Hating himself more. It took him hours to stop shaking. That night it rained. He fended off sleep, listening to the patter with his full attention, hoping its music might have something to tell him. Twice he belched up blood, then a paste of phlegm and hamburger pulp. Jesus, he thought, distantly, I'm sick. By nightfall, he was able to sit awhile and take a little soup, but he could not stand. Both his legs ballooned so tightly in his trousers he had to cut the cloth with scissors and peel it off like strips of bacon. Parts of his body were burning, refusing to obey him. He reached into his desk drawer for Morgan's application and saw straightaway that Ed Morgan couldn't spell. David smiled ruefully, looking for more faults. Morgan listed his address in Skokie, his occupation as a merchant marine, and provided no next of kin to call in case of emergencies.

That was all, and David for the life of him could not see that night, or the following morning, how he could face anyone in the studio again. Painfully, he remembered his promotion a year earlier. His teacher had held a ceremonial Buddhist candle, the only light in his darkened living room in a house near the Mission District barely bigger than a shed. David, kneeling, held a candle too. "The light that was given to me," said his teacher, repeating an invocation two centuries old, "I now give to you." He touched his flame to the wick of David's candle, passing the light, and David's eyes burned with tears. For the first time in his life, he felt connected to cultures and people he'd never seen—to traditions larger than himself.

His high school instructors had dismissed him as unteachable. Were they right? David wondered. Was he made of wood too flimsy ever to amount to anything? Suddenly, he hated those teachers, as well as the ones at Elizabeth's school, but only for a time, hatred being so sharp an emotion, like the business end of a bali-song knife, he could never hang on to it for long—perhaps that was why he failed as a fighter—and soon he felt nothing, only numbness. As from a great distance, he watched himself sponge-bathe in the sink, dress himself slowly, and prepare for Thursday's class, the actions previously fueled by desire, by concern over consequences, by fear of outcome, replaced now by something he could not properly name, as if a costly operation once powered by coal had reverted overnight to the water wheel.

When six o'clock came and only Mark, Wendell, and Elizabeth showed, David telephoned a few students, learning from parents, roommates, and live-in lovers that none was home. With Morgan, he suspected. So that's who he called next.

"Sure," said Morgan. "A couple are here. They just wanted to talk."

"They're missing class."

"I didn't ask them to come."

Quietly, David drew breath deeply just to see if he could. It hurt, so he stopped, letting his wind stay shallow, swirling at the top of his lungs. He pulled a piece of dead skin off his hand. "Are you coming back?"

"I don't see much point in that, do you?"

In the background he could hear voices, a television, and beer cans being opened. "You've fought professionally, haven't you?"

"That was a long time ago—overseas. Won two, lost two, then I quit," said Morgan. "It doesn't count for much."

"Did you teach?"

"Here and there. Listen," he said, "why did you call?"

"Why did you en*roll?*"

"I've been out of training. I wanted to see how much I remembered. What do you want me to say? I won't come back, all right? What do you want from me, Lewis?"

He did not know. He felt the stillness of his studio, a similar stillness in himself, and sat quiet for so long he could have been posing for a portrait. Then:

"You paid for a week in advance. I owe you another lesson."

Morgan snorted. "In what—Chinese ballet?"

"Fighting," said David. "A private lesson in *budo*. I'll keep the studio open until you get here." And then he hung up.

Morgan circled the block four times before finding a parking space across from Lewis's school. Why hurry? Ten, maybe fifteen minutes he waited, watching the open door, wondering what the boy (and he was a boy in Morgan's eyes) wanted. He'd known too many kids like this one. They took a few classes, promoted themselves to seventh *dan*, then opened a storefront dojo that was no better than a private stage, a theater for the ego, a place where they could play out fantasies of success denied them on the street, in school, in dead-end jobs. They were phony, Morgan thought, like almost everything in the modern world, which was a subject he could spend hours deriding, though he seldom did, his complaints now being tiresome even to his own ears. *Losers,* he thought, who strutted around in fancy Oriental costumes, refusing to spar or show their skill. "Too advanced for beginners," they claimed, or, "My *sensei* made me promise not to show that to anyone." Hogwash. He could see through that shit. All over

America he'd seen them, and India too, where they weren't called fakirs for nothing. And they'd made him suffer. They'd made him pay for the "privilege" of their teachings. In twenty years as a merchant marine, he'd been in as many schools in Europe, Japan, Korea, and Hong Kong, submitting himself to the lunacy of illiterate fak(e)irs—men who claimed they could slay an opponent with their breath or *ch'i*—and simply because his hunger to learn was insatiable. So he had no rank anywhere. He could tolerate no "master's" posturing long enough to ingratiate himself into the inner circles of any school—though 80 percent of these fly-by-night dojos bottomed out inside a year. And, hell, he was a bilge rat, never in any port long enough to move up in rank. Still, he had killed men. It was depressingly easy. Killed them in back alleys in Tokyo with blows so crude no master would include such inelegant means among "traditional" techniques.

More hogwash, thought Morgan. He'd probably done the boy good by exposing him. His own collarbone had been broken twice, each leg three times, all but two fingers smashed, and his nose reshaped so often he couldn't remember its original contours. On wet nights he had trouble breathing. But why complain? You couldn't make an omelet without breaking a few eggs.

And yet, Morgan thought, squinting at the door of

the school, there was a side to Lewis he'd liked. At first he had felt comfortable, as if he had at last found the *kwoon* he'd been looking for. True, Lewis had come on way too cocky when asked to spar, but what could you expect when he was hardly older than the high school kids he was teaching? And maybe teaching them well, if he was really going by that list of rules he handed out to beginners. And it wasn't so much that Lewis was a bad fighter, only that he, Morgan, was about five times better because whatever he lacked now in middle age—flexibility and youth's fast reflexes—he more than made up for in size and experience, which was a polite word for dirty tricks. Give Lewis a few more years, a little more coaching in the combat strategies Morgan could show him, and he might become a champion.

But who did he think he was fooling? Things never worked out that way. There was always too much ego in it. Something every *sifu* figured he had to protect, or save face about. A lesson in *budo*? Christ, he'd nearly killed this kid, and there he was, barking on the telephone like Saddam Hussein before the bombing started, even begging for the ground war to begin. And that was just all right, if a showdown—a duel— was what he wanted. Morgan set his jaw and stepped onto the pavement of the parking lot. However things went down, he decided, the consequences would be on Lewis—it would be *his* call.

Locking his car, then double-checking each door (this was a rough neighborhood, even by Morgan's standards), he crossed the street, carrying his workout bag under his arm, the last threads of smog-filtered twilight fading into darkness, making the door of the *kwoon* a bright portal chiseled from blocks of glass and cement. A few feet from the entrance, he heard voices. Three students had shown. Most of the class had not. The two who had visited him weren't there. He'd lectured them on his experience of strangling an assailant in Kyoto, and Toughie had gone quiet, looked edgy (fighting didn't seem like fun then) and uneasy. Finally, they left, which was fine with Morgan. He didn't want followers. Sycophants made him sick. All he wanted was a teacher he could respect.

Inside the school's foyer he stopped, his eyes tracking the room. He never entered closed spaces too quickly or walked near corners or doorways on the street. Toward the rear, by a rack filled with halberds and single-edged broadswords, a girl of about five, with piles of ebony hair and blue eyes like splinters of the sky, was reading a dog-eared copy of *The Cat in the Hat*. This would be the child of the class leader, he thought, bowing quickly at the portrait of the school's founder. But why bring her here? It cemented his contempt for this place, more a day care center than a *kwoon*. Still, he bowed a second time to the founder. Him he respected. Where were such grand old stylists when you needed them? He did not see Lewis, or any other student until, passing the curtained office, Morgan whiffed food cooking on a hot plate and, parting the curtain slightly, he saw Wendell, who would never in this life learn to fight, stirring and seasoning a pot of couscous. He looked like that children's toy, Mr. Potato Head. Morgan wondered, Why did David Lewis encourage the man? Just to take his money? He passed on, feeling his tread shake the floor, into the narrow hall where a few hooks hung for clothing, and found Elizabeth with her left foot on a low bench, lacing the wrestling shoes she wore for working out.

"Excuse me," he said. "I'll wait until you're finished."

Their eyes caught for a moment.

"I'm done now." She kicked her bag under the bench, squeezed past Morgan by flattening herself to the wall, as if he had a disease, then spun round at the entrance and looked squarely at him. "You know something?"

"What?"

"You're wrong. Just *wrong*."

"I don't know what you're talking about."

"The hell you don't! David may not be the fighter, the killer, you are, but he *is* one of the best teachers in this system."

Morgan smirked. "Those who can't do, teach, eh?"

She burned a look of such hatred at Morgan, he turned his eyes away. When he looked back, she was gone. He sighed. He'd seen that look on so many faces, yellow, black, and white, after he'd punched them in. It hardly mattered anymore. Quietly, he suited up, stretched his arms wide, and padded barefoot back onto the main floor, prepared to finish this, if that was what Lewis wanted, for why else would he call?

But at first he could not catch sight of the boy. The others were standing around him in a circle, chatting, oddly like chess pieces shielding an endangered king. His movements were jerky and Chaplinesque, one arm around Elizabeth, the other braced on Wendell's shoulder. Without them, he could not walk until his bruised ankles healed. He was temporarily blind in one blackened, beefed-over eye. And since he could not tie his own sash, Mark was doing it for him. None of them noticed Morgan, but in the school's weak light, he could see blue welts he'd raised like crops on Lewis's cheeks and chest. That, and something else. The hands of the others rested on Lewis's shoulder, his back, as if he belonged to them, no matter what he did or didn't do. Weak as Lewis looked now, even the old cook Wendell could blow him over, and somehow it didn't matter if he was beaten every round, or missed class, or died. The others were the *kwoon*. It wasn't his school. It was theirs. Maybe brought together by the boy, Morgan thought, but now a separate thing living beyond him. To prove the system, the teaching here, false, he would have to strike down every one of them. And still he would have touched nothing.

"Ed," Lewis said, looking over Mark's shoulder. "When we were sparring, I saw mistakes in your form, things someone better than me might take advantage of. I'd like to correct them, if you're ready."

"What things?" His head snapped back. "What mistakes?"

"I can't match your reach," said Lewis, "but someone who could, getting inside your guard, would go for your groin or knee. It's the way you stand, probably a blend of a couple of styles you learned somewhere. But they don't work together. If you do this," he added, torquing his leg slightly so that his thigh guarded his groin, "the problem is solved."

"Is that why you called me?"

"No, there's another reason."

Morgan tensed; he should have known.

"You do some warm-up exercises we've never seen. I like them. I want you to lead class tonight, if that's okay, so the others can learn them too." Then he laughed. "I think I should warm the bench tonight."

Before Morgan could reply, Lewis limped off,

leaning on Mark, who led him back to his office. The two others waited for direction from Morgan. For a moment he shifted his weight uncertainly from his right foot to his left, pausing until his tensed shoulders relaxed and the tight fingers on his right hand, coiled into a fist, opened. Then he pivoted toward the portrait of the founder. "Bow to the master." They bowed. "Now to our teacher." They did so, bowing toward the curtained room, with Morgan, a big man, bending deepest of all.

Publishing History

"Sweet Dreams," "Better Than Counting Sheep," "Cultural Relativity," "Dr. King's Refrigerator," and "The Queen and the Philosopher" were originally written for Humanities Washington, which commissions local Seattle writers to read new stories. The yearly readings have become a major Seattle literary event.

"Sweet Dreams" was first published in *Story Quarterly* 36 in 2000. It is also included in *Dark Matter II: A Century of Speculative Fiction from the African Diaspora*, which Warner Books published in January 2004.

"Better Than Counting Sheep" was published in *Callaloo* in 2001 and broadcast on radio station KUOW in Seattle.

"Cultural Relativity" first appeared in the *Indiana Review* in 2002, then a few months later as the lead story in *After Hours: A Collection of Erotic Writing by Black Men* (Plume, 2002). This story was adapted as a short film entitled "In His Kiss" by David S. De Crane.

"Dr. King's Refrigerator" was published in the fall 2003 *Story Quarterly*.

"The Queen and the Philosopher" has not been published before.

"*Kwoon*" was originally published in *Playboy* and is one of the O. Henry Prize Stories. The story was reprinted in *Playboy Stories: The Best of Forty Years of Short Fiction*, and in two high school textbooks, *A Multicultural Reader* and *Choosing to Emerge as Readers and Writers*, and *The Norton Anthology of Contemporary Fiction*.

"Executive Decision" was originally written for *Outside the Law: Narratives on Justice in America* (Beacon, 1997). It was the only work of fiction in the book. Johnson thinks it's quite possibly the only published short story that dramatizes the issue of affirmative action.

"The Gift of the *Osuo*" was published in the issue of the *African American Review* that was entirely devoted to Johnson's work.

About the Author

DR. CHARLES JOHNSON, a 1998 MacArthur fellow, is the S. Wilson and Grace M. Pollock Endowed Professor of English at the University of Washington in Seattle. His fiction includes *Faith and the Good Thing, Dreamer,* and *Middle Passage*—for which he won the National Book Award—and two short story collections, *The Sorcerer's Apprentice* and *Soulcatcher and Other Stories*. His nonfiction books include *Turning the Wheel: Essays on Buddhism and Writing, Being and Race: Black Writing Since 1970,* and two collections of comic art. In 2002 he received the Academy Award in Literature from the American Academy of Arts and Letters. He lives in Seattle.